Ellery should be free. Alpha Carter is gone, and now that the Green Hill pride has Gal, things are getting better. But Ellery is tainted by his father's attempt at killing the alpha mate, and no one will let him forget it or show that he didn't have anything to do with his father's plan.

Forest isn't in Green Hill to stay. He's doing Gal a favor by playing beta to his alpha for a while, but he's never been one to stay in one place. He can't, not unless he wants his mother to drag him home and finally seal the arranged marriage with the alpha's daughter.

Ellery isn't going anywhere, while Forest is planning to leave. But when they meet, they realize they're mates—and that something needs to change.

Ellery
Copyright © 2020 Catherine Lievens
ISBN: 978-1-4874-2802-0
Cover art by Angela Waters

Published by eXtasy Books Inc or
Devine Destinies, an imprint of eXtasy Books Inc

Look for us online at:
www.eXtasybooks.com or www.devinedestinies.com

ELLERY
GREEN HILL PRIDE BOOK 2

BY

CATHERINE LIEVENS

CHAPTER ONE

This was heaven — or rather, it would be heaven if the mosquitoes hadn't decided they needed to eat Ellery. He hoped they'd get indigestion. He hoped they *died* because of his blood.

He scratched his arm again and contemplated what to do next. He could go back inside, which was thankfully *sans* mosquitoes, but he didn't want to. He was enjoying being outside too much after spending most of the recent years locked inside the house.

The entire pride had been stuck inside, and it hadn't been easy or fun. They'd been allowed outside to a small patch of vegetables in the garden, but even that source of food hadn't been enough for the entire pride. But Alpha Carter had been convinced this was the best way to lead the pride, and everyone had followed. He was the alpha. He should have known better.

Except he hadn't, and he'd almost killed the entire pride. Ellery hadn't realized it at the time, and neither had anyone else, or if they had, they hadn't said anything. But now the pride was free, and it was weird getting used to it. It was strange to be able to leave the house whenever they wanted and even be encouraged to do so. The old alpha hadn't wanted them to work outside the pride. He'd wanted to be the one to provide for the pride, and he had, at least in the beginning. But now, Gal wanted all of them to find a job, and he'd been clear that he wanted them to enjoy what they would do.

1

That was one of the reasons Ellery was here. He wanted to find a job to help the pride. He wanted to find a job so he didn't have to stay in the house anymore. He didn't know what he could do, though.

He'd been homeschooled, like everyone in the pride, and he knew that it wasn't anywhere close to a college degree, but it was something. He could probably find a job in town, but he hadn't yet applied for anything because he didn't know what he wanted to do with his life.

He hadn't had a life until now. He'd thought he would continue to live the way Alpha Carter had made him live — locked in the house, going crazy having to share space with so many people. The only thing that had helped Ellery deal with it was patching up the house when it needed to be, which had become more frequent as time passed. He and Liam and a few others were the main reason the house hadn't crumbled down yet, and Ellery was proud of it. He just didn't know if he wanted to make a career out of it.

And wasn't that weird? He could build himself a career. Gal would support him, even after what Ellery's father had done.

Some days, Ellery couldn't believe his dad had tried to kill Gal and had almost killed Liam in the attempt. Other days, he understood how his father had been pushed to it. He didn't agree with what his father had done, of course. He liked Liam and Gal, and even if he hadn't, he wouldn't have supported it.

Ellery would always love his father, but he couldn't support a man who'd almost killed two people because he wanted to become the alpha, especially after seeing what being the alpha did to a person. Alpha Carter had ended up going out of his mind. He'd tried to kidnap Cooper after Cooper had left to live with his mate. That was the thing that had precipitated the situation, and it was the reason they had Gal now. Not that Ellery cared. Gal was a better alpha than Alpha Carter had ever been, and Ellery was grateful that Gal had met his mate and had decided to stay.

That didn't change what Ellery's father had done, though. Most of the pride was still looking at Ellery as if he'd had something to do with it. He hadn't. Of course not. He and Liam were friends, and they were becoming closer now that they were allowed to. But when they looked at him, people could only see what his father had done, and they didn't care that Ellery had nothing to do with it or that he would have stopped his father if he'd known.

"Here you are," a voice said, making Ellery jump.

His heart raced as he looked around, only relaxing when he saw Liam walking toward him. "What are you doing here?" he asked.

Liam grimaced and flopped onto the stone bench next to Ellery. "Running away from Sandra."

Ellery chuckled. "What did she do now?"

"I don't know. I ran before she could find me. But she has a lot of requests, and she thinks I should listen to her because she's an elder. I don't think she has a lot of trust in me, or in the fact that I'm the alpha mate."

"She's not used to it. None of us are."

Liam's shoulders slumped. "I'm not used to it, either. I don't know that I'll ever get used to it, to be honest. Me, the alpha mate. Who would've thought?"

Ellery thought that Liam was going to be a great alpha mate, but he didn't tell him that. He already had, and repeating it wouldn't change that fact or that Liam didn't believe him. Liam needed to trust his abilities, but he didn't yet. The time would come, though. Ellery knew it. And if Liam needed him to, he'd be right there next to him to help him face what the future held for him in the pride.

"You have to be firmer with her," he suggested.

Liam narrowed his eyes at him. "Firmer? She's going to tear my head off with her bare teeth, and I mean her human teeth, not her tiger ones."

Ellery couldn't help it—he laughed. "No, she won't. You're younger and stronger, and probably faster."

"And that's the only reason she won't hurt me? Jeesh, El. Thank you."

"No. The reason she won't hurt you is that she's afraid of the council and of being kicked out of the pride. She's demanding, but she's just trying to see if she can influence you. *That's* what she wants. That's what most of the elders want. They want to be an important part of the pride, and they want to make decisions."

Liam scowled. "They should have become alpha, then. They could have made all the decisions, and I'd be able to spend more time with my mate."

"But *Gal* is the alpha, and nothing is going to change that. That means you're the alpha mate. Sandra is harmless, but you need to be careful with what you tell her. She won't forget even one word. You know how she is. And she's going to use everything she remembers to her advantage, even if it's against you."

Liam sighed heavily and tilted his face toward the sky. He closed his eyes and basked in the sunlight, just like Ellery had done until a few minutes ago. "Being the alpha mate is so fucking hard," he muttered. "I wish I didn't have to do this."

"But then you might not have Gal, and that's not something you want to happen."

Liam opened one eye to look at Ellery. "You're right. I don't want that to happen. I'm not letting him go now that I have him."

"And things will become easier once his friend arrives, right?"

It was the talk of the entire pride. Instead of asking one of them to become the beta, Gal had asked one of his friends. Apparently, it was fairly common for groups involved with the council. The council sent alphas and betas to the shifter groups who needed them, and they helped those groups build themselves up.

The difference was that the alphas and betas usually left once that was done, but Gal wasn't going anywhere. He'd met Liam, and he'd settled down. Most of the pride agreed that Gal would be a good permanent alpha. But he needed a beta, and he'd explained that while he was proud of the progress the pride was making and how its members were behaving, he didn't think that any of them could become a beta. No one had that kind of experience, and after spending so much time under the thumb of Alpha Carter and his beta, they couldn't shoulder the job and responsibilities it implied.

So he'd called someone from outside, and a lot of pride members hadn't liked it, Sandra included. Ellery was ready to bet that was why she was hounding Liam, even though there was nothing he could do about it. He might be the alpha mate, but he didn't make those kinds of decisions. Gal did.

Ellery reached out and patted Liam's knee. "Everything is going to be okay. You just have to stand up to her, and to anyone else with something to tell you. You're the alpha mate. You should be respected, just like Gal." Ellery knew all about losing respect, and he never wanted that to happen to Liam. It was already more than enough that he was a pariah in his own pride.

He would never wish that on anyone else, not even his worst enemy — not even Sandra.

Forest wasn't sure what he was getting himself into.

He'd agreed to help Gal, so of course, he would do that. He didn't know what else Gal expected from him, though. Forest had been stunned when Gal had told him he was staying in Green Hill. Gal was like him—they moved around to groups of shifters that needed them, helped them get back on their feet, then they left again, moving on to the next group, then the next. They never stopped, not for long, and Forest liked it that way. It meant that his parents didn't have an excuse to ask him to come home, and when they did, he could tell them he couldn't because he was needed.

But that was over for Gal now. He'd found his mate, and he was sticking around in Green Hill. He was the Green Hill pride alpha now, and Forest would make sure to tease him about that. He didn't think he could stick around, though. He'd never wanted to stay anywhere. Gal was a good friend, and he knew they worked well together. They'd done so a few times, and it was always a pleasure. Even more importantly, they were friends, and Forest wanted more time with Gal. Their job wasn't amenable to keeping strong friendships, not when they moved around so often. Forest had acquaintances, of course, and he had his family back home, but that was about it, and he was happy to be here in Green Hill to see Gal.

Happy, even though Gal would expect him to work while he was here.

Of course, Forest didn't have to make a decision right now. He didn't have to stick around if he didn't want to after he was done helping Gal. But Gal knew him. There was a reason he'd called Forest of all people to help him, and Forest suspected it was because his friend could tell that Forest wanted the same—a pride, a pack, or whatever group of people he found himself comfortable with, a place where he could put down roots, maybe start a family. Instead, Forest was always moving around, and he knew that wouldn't stop. It couldn't, not if he wanted to be free to live his life the way he wanted.

He rubbed his face and did his best to focus on the road. The last thing he needed was an accident, especially one caused by him thinking about his parents and the situation waiting for him at home. It was stupid. He was an adult, and he didn't have to do the things his parents expected him to do. He didn't have to follow the path they'd set for him in life. Hell, he hadn't. He'd left home and had started this job, and even though it had started as an excuse not to get married, he liked doing it. He liked being a beta. It was a job with responsibilities, but he wasn't the one in charge. Instead, he helped the alpha, pointing out things that the alpha might not realize or understand, but he didn't have the fate of people in his hands. That was the best part of his job, and he never wanted to be an alpha.

That was precisely what would happen if he went home and did what his parents expected, which was marry the alpha's daughter.

Forest shook his head. He should stop thinking about that right now. There was no way he'd do it, and he knew his parents suspected that was the reason he was always on the move. So far, they hadn't said anything. They would eventually, but Forest would worry about that when it happened. In the meantime, he had other things to focus on, so he drove a little faster, eager to get to Green Hill and see what his home would be for the next few months, or maybe more.

Gal had given him as many details as he could, but Forest knew that he would find out a lot of things on his own. He knew the pride had been extremely isolated by their alpha. Most were forced to stay inside the house in the past few years. He could too easily imagine how that had gone. Put a large number of people in the house and forbid them to leave, and things degenerated. He was surprised no one had killed anyone, although maybe they had. He didn't have that kind of detail.

But he knew that forced cohabitation could create problems, and while he wasn't looking forward to solving them, he hoped the pride was working on getting better and back on their feet. That was why Gal was there, after all. Although, he'd admitted on the phone that he had a lot of work untangling the accounts and what the old alpha had done for the pride to survive. With no one leaving the house and having a job, the man had had to find money in some way, and Forest suspected not all those ways had been legal. Gal was on the case now, of course, but that didn't mean everything was okay. It would take time, and that was one of the reasons Forest was there.

He held his breath when he got to the gate. He expected a rundown house since no one had been able to do much for the outside since they hadn't been allowed, but Gal was already working on it. Forest leaned over the wheel and peeked at the roof, where two people were walking around, fixing it. The house also looked like it had just gotten a fresh coat of paint, and it gleamed white in the sunlight.

When Forest looked closer, he could see some spots where it still needed to be fixed. There was a window that appeared broken, and the door also needed to be painted. The porch sagged just a bit, but it was still standing, and hopefully, that wouldn't change anytime soon.

But the house looked good, and it would look even better once the people working on it were done. Hopefully, these were professionals rather than pride members, because Forest suspected that none of them had that kind of ability, not yet anyway. Maybe one of them had decided that they wanted to make it their job, and that would be good. But it would take a while for them to train, and the pride needed to be safe in the meantime.

Forest opened the window and reached out to push the button on the intercom. He had to wait a while for someone to answer, but when they finally did, they opened the gate without hesitation. Forest was grateful. He'd been in the car for a while, and he couldn't wait to get out and stretch his legs.

He parked the car next to the ones already in front of the house, then got out and looked up at the place that would be his home for the next few months. He stretched, raising his arms, smiling at the crack in his spine. He was happy to be here, even though he didn't know what the future would look like and if it would happen here.

The house was smallish, and Forest wasn't sure how many pride members there were, but he hoped it wasn't too many. It was a worry, though. Even though people were now leaving the house and going into town, working jobs, not all the pride members had found something to do, and they were still stuck in here. It meant the situation could be explosive, especially after what had happened to Gal and his mate when Gal had first arrived. Someone hadn't wanted him there, and they'd tried getting rid of him, hurting his mate in the process. People were bound to hold grudges about that, and only time would tell what they would do and whether they would try to retaliate. Forest hoped they wouldn't. Rebuilding the pride was already a lot of work, and the last thing they needed was someone working actively against them. But it wouldn't be the first time something like that happened, and Forest and Gal knew what they were doing. Still, the house was small for a big group of people, and it was worrying.

But that was Forest's job. It was his life. It was what he did and what he was good at. Gal had asked him to come for a reason, and he wouldn't let his friend down. He never had, and he wouldn't start now.

He was ready to face this new situation head-on.

Ellery and Liam heard the car at the same time. They looked at each other, and Ellery arched a brow in question. Liam shrugged, but he rose from the bench and took his hand, dragging him along.

"Are you expecting someone?" Ellery asked as he followed Liam. Not that he had a choice. Liam wasn't letting go, and Ellery knew what he was doing.

He was the first to admit he'd closed himself off from other people since his father had been arrested. Most of the pride members didn't want anything to do with him anyway, and he didn't blame them, not entirely. But the fact that he hadn't helped his father and that he hadn't known what his dad was planning made the situation more hurtful. The pride should be his family, and they should support him, especially after he lost both his parents. Instead, they treated him like a pariah, as if *he'd* been the one to attack Liam and Gal.

He shook his head. He didn't want to spend more time with the pride members, but he couldn't say no to Liam. They were each other's only friend, and Ellery cared for him. He knew Liam's new life was hard on him, and he wanted to help any way he could. If that meant spending more time with Liam and facing the other pride members, then that was what he would do.

"I don't know. People are working on the roof and repainting the house, but I thought they'd already arrived."

Ellery peered around Liam. The gate had opened to let in a car, then closed again. "Well, it doesn't look like it's someone who's here to work on the house. I mean, it looks like a normal car, not a truck." Liam stopped at the edge of the woods and peered at the house—and at the car that had stopped in front of it. Ellery rolled his eyes, but he followed Liam's lead, leaning against a tree and peeking out. "You do know that you're the alpha mate, right?" he asked in a whisper.

Liam glared at him, but Ellery could see he wasn't angry. "I'm aware of that, thank you."

"That means you should probably go out there and

welcome whoever that is. I mean, if Gal can't do it on his own, you're the next best thing. Or do you want Sandra to snatch your job?"

Liam shuddered. "The pride would be a mess if she had any kind of power. I'm going to go out there and welcome whoever it is. At least Sandra won't bug me if I'm talking to someone. Or if I'm hiding in the bushes. That's not a bad idea, actually. I won't have to talk to anyone if I hide in the bushes."

"You're going to have to talk to her and meet people you don't like eventually. It's part of your job," Ellery pointed out.

"Stop making so much sense and spy on this guy with me."

They did. The man who left the car was gorgeous—tall, definitely taller than Ellery, with bright red hair that made Ellery think that he probably had freckles, too. His skin was pale, and he glowed in the sunlight. Ellery wished he could see the man's eyes, but since he couldn't, he focused on the round ass under the jeans and on the flat stomach the man had exposed when he'd stretched his arms.

Ellery sucked in a breath. "Who is it?" he asked, his voice slightly strangled.

Liam shot him a smirk as if he knew what Ellery was thinking. "I'm pretty sure that's Gal's friend, Forest. He's a wolverine shifter, you know."

It took Ellery a moment to realize who Liam was talking about. "You mean he's the new beta."

"Exactly. I *think* it's Forest, the guy Gal wanted to come here to help." He frowned. "From what Gal told me, he's not a guy to stop in one place. He'll leave eventually, as soon as Gal has things under control."

Ellery frowned. "Why are you telling me this?"

"Because you look interested."

Ellery shook his head. "Don't worry. I have no intention of starting anything with him or with anyone else." He knew better.

Even though Forest was gorgeous and Ellery's first instinct was to walk up to him and start a conversation, he wasn't about to do that. He was a pariah. The pride had made sure he knew that, and they would no doubt tell Forest about it, too. They wouldn't want the beta to strike up a friendship with someone who wasn't deserving of being a pride member. Ellery knew that the only reason he was still here was that Gal and Liam were his friends. If they hadn't been — if they'd been more like Alpha Carter — he'd already have been kicked out of the pride along with his father.

He was lucky he was still here. Even though the pride hadn't felt like home or a family in a long time, it was still the only place and people Ellery knew. He didn't know what he would do if he didn't have them, even though he sometimes longed to be able to leave.

Where would he go, though? His father had done a terrible thing, and Ellery would never be able to forget it. It looked like the pride wouldn't, either. They weren't a family who loved him. They'd been more than happy to push him out when his father had revealed his true colors, and they had, too. That had left Ellery alone except for Liam and Gal, and while he was grateful for their friendship, they couldn't be at his side twenty-four seven. That meant he had to face the pride the rest of the time, which was one of the reasons why he was spending so much time on his own.

That couldn't go on forever, could it? Liam was trying to push him to have more conversations and more friendships, to spend more time with the pride. He didn't know how bad things had gotten because Ellery hadn't told him, and he wasn't planning to.

Liam and Gal had already done so much. They made sure to show the pride that they didn't have anything against Ellery. They ate with him at the table, talking to him as if he were a friend, and he knew that he was. But they both had their jobs, and they couldn't protect Ellery forever. Eventually, something would break, and Ellery found himself wondering if maybe it would have something to do with the new beta.

The man was gorgeous. It had been so long since Ellery had felt this way about anyone that it took him a second to recognize it—he was attracted to Forest. It wasn't something that often happened, mostly because Ellery hadn't been allowed to leave the house in a while. Even now that he was, he'd only gone to town a few times, and he hadn't met anyone who struck him the way Forest had. If his life were perfect, he'd talk to Forest, and maybe they could have something. Even if Forest left eventually, not all relationships were made to last years. It could be a summer fling or something like that. It could be Ellery's first step back into the dating game.

But it wouldn't be.

Ellery couldn't allow that to happen. He knew the pride wouldn't. He could hope and dream, but that was where things stopped.

"El?" Liam asked, his voice carrying a worried tone Ellery wasn't used to hearing these days.

Ellery forced himself to smile. "What is it?"

"Are you okay?"

"Of course. Why wouldn't I be?"

"I don't know, but you don't look so good."

"I'm fine. I promise. It's just a lot to wrap my mind around, you know? Everything is changing so fast, and some days, I feel like the ground is shifting under my feet. I have to make a lot of decisions, and I don't know where to start." That was one more reason to hate the way the pride had been when Alpha Carter had led it. He hadn't allowed anyone to make their own decisions, and now Ellery didn't know how to do it.

"You know no one is going to say anything if you take a few weeks to decide what kind of job you want. We're all in the same boat here."

"You're not."

"That's because I'm the alpha mate. It's not like I had a choice." Liam glared, but Ellery knew that he wouldn't change his position for anything in the world. He might not be happy to be the alpha mate and to be in charge, but he wouldn't give Gal up for anything. He was in love with his mate, as he should be. The pride had always liked him, and that wouldn't change anytime soon.

Ellery was the only one who had to face the kind of hate they were throwing his way, and some days, he wished he could leave. Maybe he would, eventually.

He didn't know where he would go or who he would go with, but it might just be worth it not to have to face what he had to face every day.

Forest looked around once he was done stretching. A woman was standing on the porch by the open door, looking at him, and he waved, smiling. "Hello! My name is Forest. Can you tell me where I can find Liam or Gal?"

The woman stared without answering, and Forest wondered if there was maybe something on his face. Hadn't he cleaned himself well after he'd eaten? He wasn't a messy eater so that probably wasn't it.

He cleared his throat. "Hello?"

The woman—an older woman, possibly one of the elders Gal had mentioned—huffed and turned around, leaving Forest where he was. He blinked, looking at the now empty porch, and wondered what had just happened. He hadn't been rude, had he? He always did his best not to be, but with people you didn't know, you could never be sure.

"I'm going to strangle her," a voice said from behind Forest, and he turned to look at the newcomer.

Newcomers, plural, because two men were walking toward him. He didn't know either of them, but then, the only person he knew here was Gal. He raised his hand and waved again, hoping these men weren't going to ignore him.

"You can't strangle her," the other man said. Forest took a moment to look at him. He was cute, with too-long brown hair that fell in front of his eyes. He was shorter than Forest, and Forest had always liked men who were shorter than him. There was something about holding them, making them feel safe, that appealed to Forest's inner caveman. The guy was also slim and pale as if he hadn't seen enough sun in the past few months. He had to be one of the pride members, of course, so it made sense.

"Why can't I? I could kick her out, at the very least. Right? I mean, it's in the job description. I'm the alpha mate. I can kick people out."

Forest grinned. So this was Liam. Forest already liked him, and he could see why Liam and Gal were good for each other. Gal would have never said something like that, of course, but he would probably have felt the same way about the woman who'd left Forest there even though she'd seen him.

Forest grinned. "I'm Forest," he yelled out. The two men were still a bit far for comfortable conversation, but Forest didn't mind. He wanted to take his time looking at Liam's friend.

They were going to have to live together for at least a few weeks, possibly longer. Forest should probably not start anything with any pride member, but no one would blame him for looking, right? He didn't know what the pride had been like before Gal had taken over when it came to same-sex couples, but he knew Gal wouldn't accept any bigotry, including homophobia. Besides, the alpha had a male alpha mate. Surely no one would say anything about other same-sex couples?

Liam finally got to Forest and stood in front of him. He stuck his hand out, and Forest took it, still smiling. "You must be Forest," Liam said.

"You got it in one. And you're Liam, of course. I heard what you said about being the alpha mate."

Liam grimaced. "Don't remind me."

"You don't like being the alpha mate?" Forest wasn't surprised. It wasn't a job most people would take willingly. Being an alpha mate meant having a lot of responsibility, and not a lot of time for yourself. He had to deal with the same things as the beta, and Forest was glad he was here because he would be able to help Liam with his duties. From what Gal had said, Liam was new at this, so he was probably a little lost.

That was precisely why Forest was here.

"Let's just say that I wouldn't have wanted the job if it didn't come with Gal," Liam said with a smile.

He dropped Forest's hand and gestured at his friend. "This is Ellery. He's a pride member and my best friend."

Ellery blinked at Liam as if he couldn't quite believe what he'd just heard, but the expression was gone just as fast as it had appeared on his face. He turned to Forest and offered him his hand just like Liam had, and taking it meant that Forest had to step closer to Ellery. He didn't mind. Ellery was even cuter from up close, and Forest hoped that Gal wouldn't mind if he had a relationship with a pride member.

It might not be the smartest thing to do, but no one had ever said that Forest was smart.

"It's a pleasure to meet you, Ellery," Forest said, making sure to give his tone a flirty inflection.

Ellery blinked at him and leaned closer, and Forest couldn't help but grin even wider. He was into Ellery as much as Ellery was into him.

The wind picked up, and Forest pushed a strand of hair

away from his forehead.

That was when he smelled it.

In the beginning, he didn't understand what it was, but it smelled delicious — spicy and warm, like coming home. He closed his eyes for a second, enjoying the scent, then his brain restarted.

He was smelling his mate, wasn't he?

"Gal will be so happy to have you here," Liam said. He'd been speaking for a moment, but Forest wasn't listening to him.

He couldn't have even if he'd wanted to, and right now, there was nothing he wanted more than to take Ellery into his arms and make sure he was where the scent was coming from. Forest was pretty sure Ellery was his mate, but he didn't know how to ascertain it. He couldn't stick his nose against Ellery's neck, no matter how much he wanted to.

Ellery seemed to have noticed what was happening, too, and he was staring at Forest with wide eyes. Forest hesitated. He didn't want to brush Liam off, but he also couldn't ignore what was happening between him and Ellery.

"Okay, what's going on with the two of you?" Liam suddenly asked.

Forest blinked at him. He had to force himself to look away from Ellery, and he realized he was still holding his mate's hand. He couldn't let go, though. He didn't want to. "I'm sorry?"

Liam cocked his head and crossed his arms over his chest. He looked from Forest to Ellery, then at their hands. "I said, what's going on with the two of you? Neither of you is listening to me."

Forest felt a flash of guilt. He *should* be listening, because that was why he was here. Liam was technically his boss, and he'd been explaining stuff to him even though Forest hadn't been paying attention. Forest knew he wasn't about to get fired, but still. It wasn't the best first impression.

He rubbed the back of his neck. "I'm sorry. It's just that I didn't expect this."

"Didn't expect what?" Liam asked.

Forest looked at Ellery. He didn't know if Ellery wanted Liam to know they were mates. Hell, apart from his name and how cute he was, he didn't know anything about Ellery, period. How should Forest answer, though? It wasn't like he could ignore Liam's questions. Liam wasn't just his boss, he was also his best friend's mate, and Forest didn't want to start their relationship with a lie.

So he just stood there, waiting. Ellery was going to have to take the next step in this situation, even though Forest could see he was uncomfortable. There was nothing Forest could do to help, though, no matter how much he wanted to.

Ellery was Liam's friend. Ellery was the one who knew the pride and Liam. He needed to make the next decision, and Forest held his breath and waited for him to do so.

CHAPTER TWO

Ellery didn't know what to do. He hadn't expected this. How could he have?

He'd never really thought about meeting his mate. Until recently, it wouldn't have been possible because he hadn't been allowed to leave the house.

But he hadn't had to leave to meet his mate. Forest wouldn't have come if Alpha Carter had still been in charge, but he wasn't, and here Ellery was, face to face with his mate, with no idea what to do or say.

"I'm starting to worry," Liam said.

Ellery wanted to answer him, but he didn't know what Forest wanted. Would he be angry if Ellery told Liam they were mates? Did he want to keep it a secret, at least in the beginning, maybe just long enough that they could have a conversation?

"Okay, this is getting weirder and weirder," Liam said. "Forest, Gal is inside. I'll take you to his office."

Forest finally dropped Ellery's hand, and Ellery missed the contact as soon as it was gone. It was ridiculous, but he wanted Forest to continue touching him, to never stop.

That would make a lot of things awkward, though. The situation was already bad enough with Liam looking at both of them as if they'd grown a second head. Ellery knew he would have to answer questions before the day was over, and he wasn't ready for that, not yet, and possibly never. How could he tell Liam what was happening when he didn't know himself? When he didn't know what Forest wanted, or if he wanted him at all?

Ellery took a step back. "I'll go to my bedroom. I have something to do," he said.

Liam arched a brow. "You have something to do."

"I do."

"Sure you do. I'll see you later, and I'm sure Forest will, too."

He knew Ellery was lying, and of course, so did Forest. Ellery didn't care, though. He needed a few moments to himself to wrap his mind around what was happening.

He'd met his mate.

Ellery almost ran inside the house. He didn't care that a few pride members were hanging around in the entrance, trying to peek at Forest. They glared at him when he passed by them, but this time, he didn't spare them a second glance. He didn't care that they were angry at him, even though they didn't have a good reason to be. He didn't care what they thought for once because he was focused on Forest and his touch, and how his hand still tingled after being trapped in Forest's.

He ran to his bedroom, slamming the door as soon as he was inside. He locked it, just in case, then flopped onto his bed. He couldn't stay still, though. He rose from the mattress and paced the room, pulling on his hair and wondering what was next.

Forest would be here in Green Hill for a bit. He was supposed to help Gal get the pride situated, but what would happen once he was done? Would he leave or would he stay? Ellery didn't know which one he hoped for. Maybe this was his chance to leave the pride behind. He'd thought about it, but now that he might be one step closer to actually doing it, something stopped him.

The pride had been his home his entire life. It was the only home and family he'd ever known, and he didn't know if he could leave, no matter how much he wanted to. And he did. He wasn't willing to stay here when no one wanted him. He also didn't want to be pushed away, though. It would be like giving up, and he'd never been a quitter.

His father had caused this situation, and Ellery wished he could see him and tell him exactly what he thought about him and what he'd done. He would deserve nothing less.

But of course, Ellery *couldn't* see him. Even if Gal had authorized him to go to the council jail, for now, his father wasn't allowed visitors. Besides, Ellery might want to yell at him, but he didn't want to see him. He didn't want to hear the lies his father would no doubt throw his way. He didn't want to hear the explanations because they would be bad ones. His father had hurt Liam. He'd almost killed him, and that was something Ellery would never forgive him for.

He didn't want to think about his father right now, though. He didn't want to think about how the pride members were treating him. No, the only thing he wanted to focus on was Forest, but even that wasn't as easy as it should be.

Ellery didn't know what Forest wanted from him—if he wanted anything at all. He didn't know what Forest expected, either. He hadn't said anything earlier, but Ellery knew Forest had realized they were mates. That was why he'd held onto Ellery's hand for so long. It was why he'd looked shocked, just as much as Ellery was.

But Ellery couldn't ignore the fact that Forest hadn't told Liam what was happening, and he didn't like it. Of course, he'd done the same thing, so he probably shouldn't blame Forest for what had happened, or rather, what *hadn't* happened.

A knock on the door made Ellery jerk. The handle turned, but since he'd locked it, it wouldn't open. "Ellery?" Liam asked from the hallway.

Ellery relaxed until he remembered that Liam was here to

ask him about Forest. "Yes?" he answered, not sure whether or not he wanted to open the door.

"Can I come in? I need to talk to you."

"I'm fine, Liam. I promise. You don't have to hold my hand."

Liam snorted. "The only hand I want to hold is Gal's, so you don't have to worry about that. And I know you're okay. I still want to talk to you, please."

Ellery could say no, and Liam would probably leave. He wouldn't abuse his power as alpha mate. Ellery was sure of that.

But Liam was his friend, and he probably worried about him more because of that than because of his role as the caretaker for the pride. He wouldn't leave because he wanted to make sure Ellery was okay, and Ellery wanted to tell him everything because Liam was the alpha mate, but mostly because Liam was his best friend.

Ellery opened the door. He shouldn't have hesitated because it would have come to this anyway. Of course he was going to open it. He couldn't afford to push his only friend away, and he didn't want to.

Liam pushed past him as if afraid Ellery would close the door again if he didn't hurry inside. He turned to face Ellery but waited until Ellery had closed the door to ask, "What's going on?"

Ellery wanted to tell him, but not right now, not so soon. "What are you doing here? I thought you'd stay with Gal and Forest."

Liam shook his head. "Of course not. It's obvious that something is going on with you, and you're more important than a meeting. Besides, Gal will tell me about it later. You know that. I don't have to be there to know what's being talked about. It's not like I don't know what's going on with the pride anyway. Will you tell me about you, then?"

"I don't know if I should." That was the only thing stopping Ellery.

Liam flopped onto the mattress and looked at Ellery. "Should I try to guess, then? That way, you can say you never told me anything."

Ellery chuckled. It was a relief to have a few more minutes before the truth came out. "I doubt it would be seen as a good excuse, but sure. Knock yourself out and try to guess."

Liam tapped a fingertip onto his chin, making a spectacle out of it. "Well, it has something to do with Forest. And I get it. I mean, I'm mated, but I have eyes, and the ass in those jeans is perfect."

Ellery made a strangled sound. He hadn't expected the conversation to take that turn. He'd never gossiped with anyone, especially not about someone he might like, and he wasn't quite sure how to go about it. Still, he needed to try. He and Liam were friends, but he wanted them to be even closer. "I like his freckles," he admitted quietly.

Liam laughed. "Who wouldn't? He has so many of them I want to start counting them and see what number I get to."

"You wouldn't be able to count all of them."

Liam wiggled his eyebrows. "Because they're under his clothes, too, but you could. That's what's going on, isn't it? You like him."

"I can't like him. I don't even know him. I just met him."

"But you want in his pants, and from the way he was looking at you, he wants the same thing. I swear, if I hadn't been there, he probably would have thrown you against his car to have his wicked way with you."

"Of course not. It's ridiculous." But it wasn't surprising that Liam thought that was what might have happened. He would continue to think that until Ellery told him the truth.

What was Ellery supposed to do? He trusted Liam, and he wanted to talk to someone about this. Did what Forest want matter at this point, anyway? It wasn't like Ellery was forcing him to be with him or anything like that. He was doing what was right for him, and hopefully, Forest wouldn't get angry at him for this. "It's more than that."

Liam's eyes widened. "More than wanting in his pants?"

"A lot more. He's my mate, Liam."

Liam opened his mouth, then closed it with a snap. He licked his lips. "I'm sorry?"

"Forest. He's my mate."

The office was nice. It looked older than what Gal usually preferred, but Forest knew it hadn't been his until recently, so he understood. Gal had to slip into another alpha's place, and that was never easy.

Gal gestured at the chairs on the other side of the desk. "Why don't you sit down?"

"It's never a good thing when you tell me to sit down. What do you have to tell me?" Forest teased. He obeyed, though. It wasn't an order, but Gal was flustered, and Forest wasn't sure why. He was curious.

"Things could be worse," Gal said. "The pride wasn't happy about my presence in the beginning, and some of them still aren't, but most members have come to realize what I could do for them. They're okay people. I promise." He turned toward the other side of the room. "What do you want to drink?"

"Water is fine. There's no need for me to get drunk, especially this early in the day and when I'm about to start my new job."

Gal rolled his eyes. "Your new job? We're friends, Forest. I'm not going to fire you because you have a beer."

"But you're not the only one I have to make happy, and the pride members might try to get me kicked out." If they hadn't liked Gal, Forest suspected they wouldn't like him, either. He was used to this kind of situation, though. Of course, this was the first time he'd met his mate in one of the shifter groups he had to help lead, and he didn't know how that would affect what he was supposed to do. He didn't know anything right now apart from the fact that Ellery was his mate and that he'd run away as if his ass were on fire as soon as he had the chance. "Tell me about the pride."

"There's not much to say. I'm sure the council has already told you most of it."

"Of course they did, but I want to hear it from you."

"Well, there aren't a lot of pride members. We lost a few when they realized I wouldn't stop them from moving away. Most reunited with family members. That leaves us with twenty-seven adults, including you and me, and six children."

"That's a lot of people to have in one house."

"It is. There have been some fights. A few people are trying to assert their dominance over the others. They're so used to having to fight for the smallest things that they can't let go of it. Liam has been doing his best to soothe people, but it's not easy."

"What about you?"

"Well, I've been repaying debts and contacting shifter groups around here so the pride will have allies. I've also been talking with businesses in town, both to repair the house and to find jobs for the pride members. Most of the adults have one now, except for those who work in the house. Carter had organized teams for several things like babysitting, kitchen stuff, growing the food, and most of the people on those teams want to continue doing that. They feel useful, and honestly, it makes sense. It's better than having twenty-seven adults trying to cook their dinner in that kitchen. The space is what it is, and after the house is fixed, I'm planning on building several cabins in the woods. Pack territory is wide, and we should take advantage of it."

Forest had already read all of that in the file the council had given him, but it was nice to have confirmation.

Gal seemed to realize he hadn't given Forest anything to drink. "Are you sure you're good with water? Because even if you don't want anything alcoholic, and trust me, I understand why, I have other stuff. You could have a soda, or milk, or—"

Forest snorted loudly. "Water is fine, Gal." He was babbling, and that wasn't something Forest was used to.

Gal's cheeks flushed, and he got a bottle of water out of the small fridge in the corner. "Sorry."

"What's going on with you?" Forest asked as he reached out to take the bottle of water.

Gal shrugged. "I'm happy to have you here. I'm kind of hoping you'll decide to stay eventually, and I guess I am overreacting a bit."

Forest cracked open the bottle and took a drink. "You think you're going to seduce me into staying with a bottle of water?"

Gal gently kicked Forest's shin. "You know what I mean." He walked around the desk and sat in his chair. He looked at home there, and Forest couldn't deny it.

Forest settled into his chair and looked at Gal. He seemed no different than he had the last time they'd seen each other. He was still strong and tall and powerful-looking, and once again, Forest understood why he was an alpha. He also understood why Gal wanted to settle down, though, especially now that he'd met his mate.

And Forest had, too.

He sighed and rubbed his face. He wasn't sure he'd be able to think about something that wasn't Ellery. Even when he tried, Ellery's presence slithered back into his thoughts, interrupting them.

"Is something the matter?" Gal asked.

"I honestly don't know." But Forest wanted to. "How do you like living here? Why did you decide to stay? Was it only because of Liam?"

Gal leaned back in his chair. He looked thoughtful for a second, and Forest had always liked that about him. He thought about things before he said them. "It's mostly because of him, but not just. I won't deny I had been thinking about settling down for a while. I loved my job, and I still do, but it's getting tiresome to move, always meeting new people, while leaving the others behind. I wouldn't have settled down here without Liam, though. But this is his home, and these people deserve a strong alpha to guide them. I always knew Liam wouldn't leave, so I decided that this might as well be the place where I stayed. Of course, I was lucky that the pride accepted me as their permanent alpha."

"Or rather, they were lucky you decided to be the permanent alpha."

Gal narrowed his eyes. "Maybe. Why are you asking? Are you thinking of settling down, too? Did you meet someone?" His eyes widened just a bit. "Am I keeping you away from them? God, Forest, I'm sorry. I should have thought better before asking you to come. I know I can be forceful sometimes, but you should have said something. I would have understood."

Forest shook his head. "Don't worry. I don't have anyone anywhere, not the way you mean it. But I do have someone here. Ellery."

Gal cocked his head. "Ellery. As in, Liam's best friend."

"Him." Forest sucked in a breath. "He's my mate."

He didn't know how that would go down. Gal was one of his best friends, and he was a good alpha who was protective of his pride members. He always had been, and now, Ellery was one of them.

Gal blinked, seemingly unable to speak for a moment. "That's a good thing," he eventually said.

Forest laughed. "You shouldn't sound so happy about it."

Gal shook his head. "It's not that I'm not happy about it. I am. I want everyone to know the happiness I have with Liam, and Ellery is your mate. You both deserve that happiness. But you haven't answered my question, and your answer could change a lot of things. Are you thinking of settling down? Because I don't think Ellery is going anywhere, although he would be more than warranted to leave."

Forest took a moment to answer. "I don't know if I'm staying. I was never like you. I never thought about settling anywhere." Because he had a home to go back to, a family. He'd avoided them, and he didn't want to get married, especially not to the alpha's daughter, but that had always been his home.

But had it? Forest hadn't stayed with his parents for years. He still visited, of course, but he couldn't deny it didn't feel that much like home anymore. Nothing felt like home. It was his own fault for moving so often, but someone had to do this job, and he didn't mind being the one who did it. But now he wasn't the only one involved. Ellery was, too, and Forest would have to make a decision.

He bit his lower lip. "You know the situation back at home with my parents," he said slowly.

Gal grimaced. "They're still going on about that marriage?"

"You know they are. They won't stop until I tell them to their face that I'm not getting married."

"Then maybe it's time to do just that. Unless you changed your mind?"

"I haven't. I'm not getting married, not to her." He'd grown up with Marissa, and he liked her, but he wasn't about to marry her, and he was pretty sure she felt the same way about him.

"The best thing would be to speak to Ellery. Have you?"

"Nope. He ran away, and I didn't go after him. I'm pretty sure Liam did, though."

"I told you, they're friends, and Liam cares for him, especially after what happened. But you should probably talk to him, too. See what he expects from your relationship."

A relationship that wasn't anything yet. But Gal was right. Forest couldn't be the only one making decisions. He'd never had to deal with something like this, but it didn't scare him. It was just another situation he would face head-on, just like he always did.

Ellery was his mate. Forest was used to making hard decisions, and he knew that no decision would be as hard as the ones he'd have to make in his relationship with Ellery.

When someone knocked on the door, Ellery knew who it was. No one but Liam and Gal ever visited him here, and he doubted Gal wanted to speak to him right now.

Ellery and Liam looked at each other. Liam raised his hands. "I have nothing to do with this. I swear."

"I know you don't. You were here with me for the past half hour." He'd been trying to convince Ellery to give Forest a chance and to talk to him, even though Ellery already knew he was going to do that.

Well, he was going to talk to Forest. Everything else, he reserved the right to wait and see what happened.

He sighed. He wasn't sure he was ready to face Forest, but he knew there was no way out of it. He had to talk to his mate, so he strode to the door and opened. Sure enough, Forest was standing there, but he wasn't alone. Gal was there, too, and he shuffled as if he wasn't the alpha and technically the owner of everything, including Ellery's bedroom.

Ellery looked from one to the other. "Yes?" he asked, even though he knew why they were there.

"I'd like to talk to you," Forest said. "I'm sure I don't have to tell you about what."

Ellery looked around. He could already see someone peeking from their bedroom door at the end of the hallway. If he stayed inside with Forest, someone would be listening to their conversation about five seconds in.

He stepped out of the bedroom, forcing Forest to retreat. "We can talk, but not here."

Forest looked around, and the door slammed. He frowned, but thankfully, he didn't say anything. "Of course. Where do you want to go? You're the one who knows the area, so I'll follow your lead."

Ellery blinked. Forest was nothing like Beta Boyd had been, was he? Of course he wasn't. Gal wouldn't have asked him to come if he were.

Just like everyone else, Ellery had been worried when Gal first arrived. He hadn't liked the thought of having someone who wasn't a pride member lead them, especially someone who wasn't even a tiger shifter. But Gal was a good person. More importantly, in this situation, he was a good alpha. He was doing what he could for the pride, even though the pride sometimes worked against him. He wouldn't have asked a bad person to become his beta, even if only temporarily.

"You two should go take a walk," Liam said as they stepped out of Ellery's bedroom. "I'm sure the bench is empty right now. It always is."

Ellery wasn't sure he wanted to share his special spot with anyone but Liam, but what choice did he have?

"Or we can just walk around," Forest said, and Ellery was grateful. He'd noticed Ellery wasn't comfortable with sharing his bench, and he was reassuring him without being obvious about it. "I've been in my car for hours. I wouldn't mind walking around, especially with this beautiful day. You can show me around the garden."

"Of course." They looked at each other, and Ellery wasn't sure what to do next. Should he take the first step and start walking away? Or did Gal have something to tell him?

"Well, Liam and I have a meeting to attend," Gal said as he reached for his mate. He tugged on Liam's arm and dragged him along the hallway.

"A meeting? What meeting? Please, tell me we're not talking to Sandra," Liam whined.

"Shut up. Don't you see they want to be on their own?" Gal was trying to whisper, but both Ellery and Forest heard him.

Ellery's cheeks flushed, but Forest just chuckled and shook his head. "Man, I didn't expect this when Gal told me he'd met his mate."

"Didn't expect what?" Ellery asked before closing his bedroom door and locking it. He always locked it because he couldn't be sure pride members wouldn't try to get in. They wanted him out, away from the pride, and he suspected they wouldn't stop for anything to obtain that.

"He's always been very closed off, if you know what I mean. He takes his job very seriously, and he doesn't usually have a lot of help. That means he spends most of his time working, and he doesn't smile a lot. He never allowed himself to fall for anyone he worked with, and it makes for a lonely life, even between jobs. But things are different here."

"Well, he met his mate. I'm sure that has a lot to do with it. The fact that he decided to stay probably also helps him relax."

Forest looked at Ellery, and Ellery wanted to shuffle. He stood his ground, though. "Probably," Forest admitted.

He stepped to the side and gestured toward the end of the hallway. "Shall we?"

Ellery took the lead, since he was the one who knew where to go. They walked outside, and Ellery felt instantly better with the wind playing in his hair and the sun on his face. God, how he'd missed this. He didn't have to miss it anymore, though. He was allowed to go outside anytime he wanted, and he'd been taking advantage of it. He didn't want to stay inside, not with the other pride members glaring at him every time he stepped out of his bedroom.

"So, I guess we should probably talk about the elephant in the room," Forest said.

"We're not in a room," Ellery pointed out.

Forest barked out a laugh. "You're right. We're not. But we should still talk about the fact that we're mates."

The words hung between them. They were mates, and they couldn't ignore it anymore. Ellery had known since he'd met Forest, but he'd thought that Forest might want to hide it from everyone else. And maybe he did, although Ellery was pretty sure he'd told Gal.

"Why don't you tell me what you have planned?" he told Forest.

Forest frowned, but he didn't push. "What I have planned? Well, I'm here to help Gal, of course. I don't know how long it's going to take. It depends on how the pride behaves when it comes to me and my presence here."

"And once you're done and the pride settles down? What's going to happen? Will you leave?"

"I was planning to, yes. I wasn't expecting to meet you, and I'm not sure what to think about this entire situation yet. But no, I wasn't planning to stick around. I love Gal. He's one of my best friends, and I love working with him. This isn't what I'm used to, though. It's not what either of us are used to. That was part of the appeal when I accepted this job, you know? Being able to see the country, to meet a lot of different people. I've had fun over the past few years, and I didn't think it would end."

Of course. Ellery should have known Forest wasn't planning on sticking around. From the way he was talking, he already saw Ellery like a weight keeping him in Green Hill. He clearly thought that Ellery was going to demand he stay, but Ellery wouldn't. He already had more than enough problems to deal with on his own. He didn't need to have Forest on the list of that.

Forest hadn't even mentioned leaving and taking Ellery with him, and again, Ellery wasn't surprised. Forest hadn't had the time to speak to the rest of the pride, and he already thought Ellery wasn't worth it. What would happen when he finally did? They would tell him Ellery had plotted with his father to kill Gal and Liam, even though it wasn't true. They would tell him they'd always thought he was a little weird, that he kept himself apart because he thought he was better than them.

None of that was true, but Forest wouldn't know. Besides, he was already talking as if he wasn't going to stay. Ellery hadn't expected anything different, but it still hurt. His mate was the one person in the world who should have his back and who should want to be with him, but instead, Forest looked like he couldn't wait to leave Green Hill.

Ellery bit his lower lip to the point of pain, trying to keep himself in the present situation. It wouldn't do any good to let his thoughts spiral out of control. "Well, I don't expect anything from you. I never did. You can leave anytime you want, and I won't try to stop you. It's your right." And Ellery was used to being alone.

Losing Forest wouldn't change anything for him, even though it would hurt. Ellery was used to pain. He could survive this one, too.

Forest didn't like how natural it seemed for Ellery to accept that he wasn't going to stay. It was almost as if Ellery hadn't expected him to, even though they were mates. Forest wanted to explain, but he wasn't sure how. Still, he needed to. He didn't want Ellery to think that he didn't care about him or that he was dismissing him. He wasn't. But his life had turned around with one meeting, in just one second, and he needed some time to wrap his mind around it and redirect what he thought his future would be.

He cleared his throat, trying to put those thoughts into words. "This isn't what I'd planned. I won't lie to you," he said. "But it doesn't mean that things have to go that way. I'm not saying I'm going to stay, but I'm also not saying I'll leave. Everything is up in the air right now."

"I told you. I understand, and I don't expect anything from you," Ellery said without looking at Forest. He was actively looking away from Forest, avoiding his gaze. Forest didn't like it.

"I understand that, but I'm trying to say that even though I planned to leave eventually, I wasn't expecting to meet my mate. I wasn't expecting to meet you, but I did. I'm going to have to learn to deal with this, and you have to do the same."

Ellery finally looked at Forest, even if it was only for a moment. "You don't have to learn to deal with me if you don't want to. You can ignore me while you're here, and when you leave, I won't try to stop you. I already told you that."

"Yes, you don't expect anything from me. I got that, and I don't like it."

That finally got Ellery's attention, and he looked Forest in the eyes. "What do you mean?"

Forest wasn't sure how to explain. He raked a hand through his hair, pulling on the strands, wondering if Ellery was going to get offended. "I don't want you to expect anything from me. We don't know each other. But you should at least want to try to build something with me."

Ellery stopped in his path and turned to face Forest. "Why should I? You just said that you're probably going to leave once you're done. Why should I want to build a life with you when you obviously don't want one?"

This was frustrating, and Forest hated that for once, he couldn't use his beta position to deal with it. He couldn't order Ellery to do anything. Ellery was his mate, and he would just tell Forest to fuck off, or at least, Forest hoped he would. He didn't want Ellery to think he had to obey him just because he was the beta. He had to follow the rules Gal and Forest would lay down, of course, but their private life was different, and Forest would never order Ellery around in a private setting.

Forest stopped in front of Ellery. "Why don't we start from the beginning? I have no idea what I'm doing. That much, I'm sure of. I was planning to leave eventually, but I didn't know about you. Now that I've met you, it's obvious that my plans are going to have to change. I'll have to factor you into anything I decide, and I'm aware of that. That's only if you want me in your life, though. If you don't, whether because you think I'll eventually leave you behind or for whatever other reason, you have to tell me. I can't start building a life around you if you're not going to be in it. You've been trying to push me away from the first moment, and I don't know what's going on. If you don't like me, that's okay. But if you have another reason, like maybe not wanting to get hurt when I leave, then please, tell me. I don't know if I'm going to leave. It's what I usually do, but again, I've never met my mate in any of the shifter groups I spent time with. My situation is pretty much what Gal's was when he met Liam, and he stayed. He's your alpha now. Don't you think the same could go for me?"

"You're right. Gal stayed. But I'm not Liam, and you're not Gal. Things will be different with us."

"Maybe they will, maybe not. You can't know that."

Ellery crossed his arms over his chest. "But don't you see? I *can* know that. I know my history. I already know what's going to happen. You're going to find out—" He snapped his mouth shut, then continued, "You're not going to want me for much longer. That's why I'm not giving you the benefit of the doubt. Because I know that you will see the truth and that you won't want to be here with me."

Something had happened to Ellery. That much was obvious, and Forest would have to talk to Gal about it. He could already tell that if he asked Ellery, his mate wouldn't tell him. Whatever it was, though, it had left him feeling like he wasn't worth having his mate in his life, and Forest didn't like it.

He didn't know what would happen, or why he'd met Ellery now, but he believed in the story that mates met for a reason. There had to be a reason all of this had happened now. Forest would find out eventually, but it would be easier if Ellery didn't push him away.

"I want to get to know you," he told Ellery.

Ellery shook his head. "Trust me. You don't."

"What have you done that's so terrible that I wouldn't want you? Have you killed someone in cold blood? Have you tortured children or kittens?"

Ellery's cheeks flushed. "Of course not."

"Then I don't see a reason not to want you. Whatever you're thinking, it can't be as bad as you think. You can tell me if you want, but I can already tell you don't, and that's okay. That's going to be a part of getting to know you. But don't think I'm going to push you away just because you believe that's what's going to happen. You don't know me. You don't know how I'm going to react."

Ellery rubbed his face, and he looked more tired than he had before. It was almost as if his vitality had leaked out of him as soon as he'd started thinking about whatever he was hiding, and Forest wished he could fix things, that he could make things better for him. He didn't know how, though. He didn't even know what was happening.

"I guess I might as well tell you. You know what happened to Gal and Liam, right?"

Forest blinked. "You mean when Liam was attacked?" Gal had told him about it, but he hadn't gone into details. Forest suspected he'd mentioned it mostly because he wanted Forest to come, and that was okay. Forest would have even if Gal hadn't asked him to, especially after finding out his best friend had been attacked. But both Gal and Liam were okay, and the man responsible was in jail.

"Yes. Liam was attacked and almost strangled to death. The man who did it wanted to hurt Gal, to get rid of him so he could become the alpha in his place." Ellery sucked in a breath and took a step away from Forest as if he were afraid that Forest was going to hurt him. "That man was my father."

Forest waited for Ellery to continue, and when he didn't, he asked, "So?"

Ellery's gaze snapped up to Forest's. "What do you mean, *so*? My father tried to kill Gal. He hurt Liam."

"I don't see what that has to do with you, though."

"How can you not?" Ellery gestured toward the house. "Everyone knows. Everyone pushes me away because of what my father did. They think I had something to do with it."

"Did you?"

Ellery shook his head vehemently. "Of course not. Liam is my best friend, and even if he wasn't, I wouldn't do anything to hurt him, Gal, or anyone else. I don't care who the alpha is as long as it's a good one, and Gal is."

"Then, again, I don't see what that has to do with you. What your father did was horrible, but you just said you had nothing to do with it."

Ellery's shoulders slumped. "The entire pride except for Liam and Gal have been holding it against me since my dad did what he did. They've been pushing me away and not speaking to me, whispering behind my back. They're going to tell you about it, and they're going to lie to you. They'll tell you that I helped him or something like that, maybe that I'm still plotting to kill Liam and Gal and that it's the only reason I'm friends with them. I don't know what they'll tell you, but I know they'll lie."

"And I won't believe them." If there was something Forest didn't like, it was liars, especially in cases like this one.

He wouldn't allow people to gossip about Ellery, especially when he hadn't done anything. He believed Ellery when he said that he wouldn't have helped his father. Liam and Gal wouldn't be his friends if he were a bad man, and that was enough for Forest to trust him. He would have to do something about the pride, though. He couldn't order them not to gossip or to leave Ellery alone, but having that kind of tension in the pride—having people so ready to talk badly about people behind their back and isolate them—didn't bode well.

It was nothing Forest hadn't already faced, though. It would be hard work, but if it meant that Ellery was happy once Forest was done, Forest was ready to give all of himself to this job.

CHAPTER THREE

Ellery didn't know what to do. He didn't know what he wanted, either, and that made everything harder.

Forest had stayed away from him since that first day, but Ellery knew it wasn't because he wanted to, but rather because he had so much work to do. He'd been talking to every single pride member, getting to know them, and asking them what they expected from the pack and what they wanted from life. Most pride members had already softened toward him. He was an authoritative figure, but he wasn't like Gal, who was more private and focused on keeping up with the demands of the house and the many people who lived there, in keeping a good relationship with the town and the nearby shifter groups, and sorting out the accounts and the mess Alpha Carter had made of them. Gal also had to deal with the council, but Forest could focus on the pride members and their needs.

He was helping Liam with his new alpha mate job, and everything was running smoother than before. He was doing a good job, and Ellery was both grateful and hesitant. If Forest was that good at being a beta, he would help put the pride back into shape soon. Then, he would leave.

Ellery wouldn't, though. Ellery would stay behind, and he'd lose his mate.

Ellery huffed at his thoughts and got up from his bed. He still hadn't made a decision when it came to Forest, even though he'd been thinking about his mate nonstop. He didn't know what Forest wanted, either. They hadn't had time to talk, and Ellery didn't know if it was because Forest was so busy or because he was staying away. Ellery knew that by now, the pride members who hated him the most had no doubt gotten to Forest. They'd told him what they thought about him, and they'd lied. Ellery had warned Forest that would happen, but there was nothing else he could do. He couldn't influence Forest's decision to believe them or not. He wished he could, but this was the reality of it, and he had to deal with it.

Maybe Forest was giving Ellery time to think about everything and make a decision. He'd told Ellery that he wanted them to get to know each other in the hope that eventually, they would become a couple and decide together what the next step would be in their life. That would be hard to do if some of the pride members tried to influence him, though, and Ellery knew they would — if they hadn't already. Ellery had waited, unwilling to get himself in trouble, but he was done. Forest wasn't the only one in this relationship. Ellery was a part of it, too, and that meant that he could take the next step as much as Forest could. He *wanted* to take the next step, but he didn't know how to do that.

He'd been sheltered. Alpha Carter hadn't done it because he wanted to keep Ellery safe. He'd held the entire pride prisoner at the end, but even before he'd made sure to isolate them, to the point that only a few of them had found their mate. Liam was one of the lucky ones, and now, Ellery was, too. Ellery had decided that he didn't want to miss this chance. He only had one mate, and it was Forest. The choice wasn't hard to make, not when Ellery considered what he would lose if he told Forest no and if he let Forest leave without him. Ellery still didn't know whether or not Forest was staying, but he'd decided that if Forest wasn't, he would go with him.

Of course, they had to become something more than

acquaintances first. Sharing a mate bond didn't make them close, and Ellery wanted to get to know his mate. They might be perfect for each other, but they would never find out if they never talked.

He didn't know where to start. He could probably ask Liam, but Liam was busy, and he was the only friend Ellery had. That meant Ellery was on his own, and he hesitated. He should do something nice for Forest, but what? What could Forest need that Ellery could provide? Ellery had no idea, but he'd noticed a pattern. When Forest was working, he rarely took the time to eat lunch. When he did, he limited himself to eating something fast, some days without even sitting down. He'd taken over supervising the renovation of the house, and he was always on the move. If he wasn't speaking to a pride member, he was climbing all over the roof or digging in the garden. He seemed to be everywhere at once except for Ellery's life, and Ellery wanted that to change.

That was what he would do. Since it was almost lunchtime, Forest would probably need something to eat, and Ellery wouldn't be surprised if he skipped lunch again. That couldn't be good for him, and while he might not be happy about Ellery's intervention, Ellery hoped the food would help smooth that over.

Ellery left his bedroom, for once not headed outside. When he was in the house, the only place where he went was usually the dining room for meals. He'd tried helping in the kitchen once, but the people there had been clear that they didn't want him anywhere near the food. They were in charge of the meals, and he shouldn't interfere. He was a traitor, after all. He might taint their food or something like that.

It was ridiculous, but Ellery didn't want to fight. Besides, he wasn't sure he would be any good at cooking. As long as they didn't starve him, he was more than happy to stay away from the stoves.

Some things still worked like they had when Alpha Carter had been in charge. He'd assigned the pride members specific jobs, and they still stuck to them. A small group worked in the kitchen, taking care of food preparation for the entire pride. Another group took care of the garden and the patch of vegetables that grew there, others maintained the cars, even though they didn't use them often. Some people babysat and taught the few children that were part of the pride. Ellery and Liam and a few others had taken care of the house as much as they could, considering how little resources they'd had.

But that was over now. Ellery couldn't work on the house anymore because professionals were doing it, and he was at a loss as to what to do. He still hadn't decided what kind of career he wanted. It felt like an impossibly big decision to make, especially since he didn't know much about the world outside the house.

He peered into the dining room, and when he saw it empty, he went into the kitchen. He held his breath, praying it would be empty, and for once, he was lucky. No one was there, but the back door was open, and he could hear voices.

He hesitated. He didn't want to face the wrath of the kitchen team. They would be angry if they saw him there, even though he had as much right as anyone else. The kitchen team took care of cooking three meals per day, but that didn't mean the pride members couldn't eat outside of those meals. Everyone was welcome to whatever was in the fridge as long as they made a note if they finished something so it could be replaced. Ellery had avoided the kitchen because he didn't want to fight, but maybe he should push. He hadn't done anything wrong. He shouldn't be barred from the communal areas of the house.

He was still frightened when he stepped into the kitchen. He rushed to the fridge, intent on hurrying so he wouldn't get caught. He didn't know how to cook, and even if he had, he didn't have time, so he limited himself to putting together a sandwich. He hoped it would be enough for Forest, and since he wasn't sure, he added a small bowl of cherry tomatoes, a piece of watermelon he found in the fridge, and an apple. It wasn't much, but it was something, and he hoped Forest would enjoy it.

"What are you doing here?"

Ellery briefly closed his eyes. He didn't want to face Anne. She was the worst, and of course, she was the one who'd found him.

"I asked you what you were doing here," she snapped.

"I'm making lunch for Forest," Ellery answered without looking at her. He grabbed the tray he'd put together and turned to leave, but she stepped into his path, crossing her arms over her chest and glaring at him.

Ellery didn't want to fight. He didn't want to create trouble, but he also wasn't going to let Anne run him out of the kitchen.

"That's not yours to take," she said.

"Of course it is. I'm a pride member."

She snorted. "Only because you're sucking up to Liam. You would have been kicked out along with your father if it weren't for him. If I were in Galbraith's shoes, I wouldn't have hesitated. He's too good. After what you did, you shouldn't even be allowed to breathe the same air as them."

Ellery sucked in a breath and put down the tray before he dropped it. "I had nothing to do with what my father did."

"No one believes that, no matter how many times you repeat that lie."

"I'm not lying." It was a moot point, though. She wouldn't believe him.

"You're a traitor," Anne said. There was so much venom in her voice that Ellery wanted to run away. "You shouldn't be allowed to stay with us. You shouldn't be allowed near our children. You shouldn't—"

"Enough."

Ellery had never been so relieved to see Helga. He looked at her, and she waved him toward the exit. "Go. I'll take care of Anne."

"You'll take care of me?" Anne asked indignantly. "What does that mean? You have no right—"

Ellery didn't wait to listen to them fight. He rushed out of the kitchen, unsure what would happen next. Helga was more than able to stand up to Anne and any other pride members, but how long would she be willing to do it for Ellery? And what would Ellery do once she'd had enough?

Forest was relieved to be interrupted by a knock on the door. He hated spending time in the office, even though some days, it was necessary. He'd much rather be outside working on the roof or talking to people.

"Come in," he called out.

The door slowly opened, and he waited to see what was going on. He kind of hoped it was Ellery because they'd barely had time to talk, and he couldn't wait to spend some time with his mate. These were the early days, though. He wasn't surprised that he didn't have time to do anything, let alone talk to his mate and get to know him. He wasn't sleeping enough, and he was skipping meals. Hopefully, things would slow down in a few days, once he finished talking to the pride members and he got a good handle on what was going on and what needed to be done. He thought he already had one, but he needed to be sure. The last thing the pride needed was for him to make a mess.

It wasn't Ellery, though. It was Helga, and Forest flopped back into his chair. "Helga. What can I do for you?" She was one of the elders—one of the good ones. She'd been important when Gal had first arrived, and Forest didn't mind her presence in the office or talking to her.

Still, he wished she were Ellery.

She stepped inside. She was holding a tray, and she slammed the door shut with her foot, making Forest jump. He wasn't sure what was happening, but he didn't like it when Helga stomped toward his desk and dumped the tray onto it.

"Did I miss something?" he asked. He wouldn't be surprised if he had. He hadn't been here long enough to know everything that was happening with the pride.

She huffed and crossed her arms over his chest. "Nothing, or maybe everything."

"That's not very clear." He looked down at the tray, surprised to see a sandwich and some fruit and vegetables. "You didn't have to bother. I could have gone to the kitchen to find something to eat."

"Oh, I didn't bother. Trust me. You're old enough to get your own lunch if you're hungry. No. This is Ellery's work."

Forest blinked. "Ellery?"

"You know. The cutie who always looks at you like he wants to eat you."

Forest chuckled. "I know who Ellery is." Neither of them had told anyone besides Gal and Liam they were mates, apparently. Forest didn't have anyone to tell since he didn't know the pride members well, and he'd noticed Ellery spent a lot of time away from everyone else. Forest didn't like it, but he hadn't had the time to address the situation yet.

"Well, he decided to bring you lunch, but he was stopped in the kitchen."

"What do you mean, he was stopped?"

Helga stared at Forest for a moment before asking, "What do you know about the situation here? About what happened to Liam and what Ellery's father did?"

"I know he was the one who tried to kill Liam, or rather,

who almost strangled Liam to death in the attempt of killing Gal."

"It's part of the story."

"I also know that some of the pride members think Ellery had something to do with it."

Helga arched a brow. "You don't think he did?"

Forest leaned back in his chair. "Liam and Gal both trust him. They wouldn't if he had anything to do with what happened. So yes. I trust him, just as much as they do."

Helga relaxed, even though Forest could see she was still angry. "You need to talk to him and the rest of the pride. This can't go on."

Forest knew he wouldn't like what he was about to hear. "Can you give me more details? I don't want to overstep, but Ellery won't talk to me. I need to know more."

"Most of the pride members have been isolating him. I don't think all of them truly believe he helped his father, but they don't want to make an enemy out of other pride members. Some of them have too much power. They shouldn't."

"Who are you talking about?" Forest had a pretty good idea. He wasn't blind, and talking to everyone meant that he had a general idea of how the hierarchy in the pride worked.

The pride members were divided into groups who took care of different aspects of everyday life. One of the more essential jobs was cooking. Cooking for the entire pride meant having control over the pride members — what and when they ate — that not many other people had. Forest hadn't said anything about it so far, but it looked like he might have to.

"Anne is one of the worst," Helga explained. "I don't like to talk badly of people behind their back, but what she and the others are doing to Ellery isn't right. He didn't have anything to do with what happened to Liam. He wouldn't still be here otherwise. But Anne and a few others are angry and resentful, and they're taking it out on him."

"What did they say today?"

"That he was a traitor. That he didn't belong with the pride. That's why you should talk to him."

Forest took a deep breath so he wouldn't snap at Helga. It wasn't her fault, and she was doing the right thing by talking to Forest. "I'll talk to him, and to Anne," he said. But he knew he couldn't be the one who did all the work.

He'd seen this kind of situation before. Even if he talked to the pride members, they would go back to their behavior as soon as he turned around. The one who had to stand up for himself was Ellery. It was his right to live here with the pride, and he needed to stop hiding in fear. Forest wanted to protect him, to shelter him, but he couldn't do that forever, even if he decided to stay in Green Hill.

"Thank you," he told Helga.

She nodded at him. "Don't worry about it." She hesitated. "Take care of him. He deserves someone who loves him."

Forest frowned. "I never said anything about loving him."

"Who do you think you're fooling? I have eyes. I know you like him."

"I do." It wouldn't help to deny it. There wasn't a reason to, either. Forest wasn't about to tell Helga that he and Ellery were mates, but he knew that even if he did, she wouldn't tell anyone. She just wasn't that kind of person.

He got out of his chair and took the tray, having decided to find Ellery so they could have lunch together. It wouldn't be a lot, since the tray had only been packed for one person, but it was better than letting Ellery starve because he didn't want to go to lunch. Forest wouldn't blame him if he avoided the kitchen and dining room today considering what Helga had told him.

"You'll probably find him outside. He likes to garden and hides in the bushes. No one bothers him there," Helga said.

Forest smiled at her. "Thank you."

"No. Thank *you*. You and Gal are doing a lot here, and I never thought I'd see the pride and the house in this state."

Forest didn't yet like where the pride was. He knew not everyone could always get along, and he didn't expect that to happen. He also didn't expect the amount of gossiping and badmouthing, though. He didn't like it, and he wanted to change it, but he knew it would take time and work.

"I know the pride isn't easy to deal with," Helga continued. "Things will never be easy. I don't envy you your job."

Forest couldn't help but smile at that. "Some days, I wish I didn't have to do it, but I signed up for it." And it had brought him Ellery. He didn't think he would ever regret the decision.

He hadn't yet decided whether or not he would stay, but he didn't fool himself into thinking that he would be able to leave Ellery behind. If Forest left, it would be with his mate.

But of course, to make that happen, he had to talk to him first.

Ellery was weak. After what had happened in the kitchen with Anne, he couldn't deny it. Instead of talking back, he'd abandoned Forest's lunch and had fled. He was hiding, something a stronger person wouldn't have done.

So yes, Ellery was weak, and he didn't know what to do about it.

He was the one who allowed this to continue. He knew he shouldn't, but it was hard, and he hated feeling alone against the world, even though that wasn't the case. He knew he wasn't alone. He had Liam at the very least, and that meant a lot to him. He also had Gal, and he was pretty sure that if he allowed Forest in, he would have him, too. Helga seemed to be on his side, but he hadn't stuck around to make sure of it. Instead, he'd run, and now, he was on his bench where no one would be able to find him.

He didn't know what to do. He wanted to fight back, but could he? Even if he told Anne the truth, even if he stood up to her and the others, that wouldn't change what they thought about him. It wouldn't change the fact that they looked at him with hatred in their eyes, and they thought he shouldn't be here. He wasn't sure if they really believed he'd helped his father hurt Liam, but he hated that they could believe that of him. He'd never done anything wrong. If anything, he'd helped several pride members over the years, fixing things in their bedrooms and bathrooms, babysitting some of the children. And this was the way they thanked him—by pushing him away and thinking he was a criminal.

He rubbed his face. If he could leave right now, he would. But he only had the clothes on his back. He didn't know how to drive, and he didn't have a car. And where would he go? He didn't have anyone else. He only had the pride, and that had been the case since he was born. It wouldn't change anytime soon, no matter how they behaved with him.

"Here you are," someone said.

Ellery jumped off the bench, ready to send whoever it was away or to leave if they wouldn't. He'd left the kitchen because he hadn't wanted to be insulted, but this was his secret spot. He wouldn't let anyone ruin it for him, not even Anne.

But it wasn't Anne. Ellery should have realized that since the voice had been a man's, but he'd been panicking. It was Forest, and he was holding the tray Ellery had put together for him.

Ellery looked at it, blinking. His eyes burned, even though he didn't understand what was happening. "How did you find me?" he asked.

Forest settled onto the bench and patted the spot beside him. Ellery sat cautiously, even though he knew Forest wouldn't hurt him. He wasn't the kind of man to do that. He was nothing like Beta Boyd had been, and Ellery couldn't have been happier about that.

"Helga told me where to find you," Forest said.

"I thought only Liam and I knew about this spot." It had been Cooper's, but Cooper had left when he'd met his mate. Ellery wished he could have gone with him, but if he had, he wouldn't have met his mate.

"I think Helga knows a lot more than she says," Forest said. He took one of the cherry tomatoes and held it out to Ellery.

Ellery shook his head. "It's your lunch. I prepared it for you."

Forest grinned. "And I thank you for that, but it doesn't mean you can't share with me. Did you have lunch already?"

Ellery's thoughts flashed back to what had happened in the kitchen. There was no way he was going back, not even to eat lunch. "No." He didn't lie because he knew Forest would realize he wasn't telling the truth. He might as well be honest.

Forest's smile widened. "See? You can share with me."

"But it's not much. I mean, I could probably have come up with something else, but I don't know how to cook, and I didn't want to set fire to the kitchen or something like that."

To Ellery's surprise, Forest reached out and gently squeezed the back of his neck. Ellery froze, his eyes wide, but Forest's hand was gone before Ellery could say anything. "This is enough," Forest said. "And thank you. I didn't expect this from you, and I'm grateful you thought about me. I won't say you shouldn't have because you know that I wouldn't have eaten lunch if you hadn't, so I'm just going to say thank you. Oh, and *please, share with me*. It might not be a lot, but I can go to the kitchen and eat more once we're done here."

Forest wasn't wrong. This was all Ellery would have as food for now since he had no intention of going back inside. He took the cherry tomato and popped it into his mouth. The fresh juice inside the tomato squirted on his lips when he bit down. He licked his lips, and he didn't miss the way Forest looked at him, his gaze dropping to his mouth.

Forest wanted him. Ellery was pretty sure that was what was happening, and he didn't know how to deal with it. He didn't know a lot of things, and he hated it.

"So, Helga talked to me," Forest said after a while. He carefully looked away from Ellery as he spoke, but Ellery knew what he was talking about.

"I don't want to talk about it."

"I just wanted to know if you were okay."

"I don't know." Physically, Ellery was perfectly fine. Anne hadn't touched him. She just had said things to him — things that hurt more than they should have.

Ellery already knew what most of the pride thought about him. He didn't understand why they thought that way, and at this point, he didn't think it mattered. He had no intention of trying to change their minds. If they thought he was a criminal, a man who hurt people, then he didn't want to be their friend.

But they were his family. They were the only people he had ever known and the only people he had in his life. Nothing could change that, and it hurt that they didn't believe him.

They were supposed to be the people who helped him back up when he fell. Instead, they were the ones pushing him down, and Ellery didn't know what to do about it. Standing up for himself would be a start, but he didn't think it would change anything. The support he had from Liam, Gal, and Forest wouldn't, either. They couldn't order Anne and the others to believe Ellery.

"I'll be fine," Ellery continued, even though he didn't know if that was the truth. "It's nothing I haven't already gone through time and time again."

"You shouldn't have to go through it."

Ellery snorted and snatched another cherry tomato from the tray. "If I could avoid it, I would. No one wants to go through something like that. But I have no idea what happened, and no one will tell me." He sucked in a breath. "But it's not your problem. I appreciate what you're doing, but you don't have to."

Forest finally looked at Ellery again. "I do. It's not just the fact that I'm the beta and that I don't like this kind of situation. It's also that you're my mate, and I want you to be happy, which you clearly aren't."

Ellery swallowed. He couldn't deny that, but even if he admitted he was unhappy, what would happen? He was stuck here. He didn't have another place to go, and just the thought of leaving made him panic, even though he knew it would be the best thing for him to do.

So what was next? The future was like a dark hole, full of unknown, terrifying things. Ellery would rather stay where he was than throw himself into that hole, even with Forest's help.

Forest hated how down Ellery was, but there was only so much he could do.

He cleared his throat. "You should stand up for yourself."

Ellery scowled at him, then stole another cherry tomato. "Don't you think I haven't thought about that?"

Forest pushed the bowl with the cherry tomatoes closer to Ellery so he could take more. "I'm sure you have."

"But I didn't today. That's what you mean. That I was a coward and ran instead of standing up to Anne and telling her what I thought of her."

Forest shook his head. "I could never think you're a coward. You and the rest of the pride went through a lot, and it's normal that you're still trying to find your footing in life. I never expected this to be smooth sailing. I'm not surprised there are snags in the plans, but that's what I'm here for. I'll try to smooth them out and help as much as possible. That includes what's happening to you."

Ellery shook his head. "It's a private situation. It has nothing to do with you or with the way the pride is led. It doesn't change anything for you."

Forest took a bite of his sandwich and carefully considered his next words. "But that's not true. I'm not even talking about the fact that you should stand up for yourself. You're not alone, and I think you know that by now. I can help, and so will Liam and Gal."

"No one can force the pride to listen to me and to accept me," Ellery snapped. His cheeks flushed, and he looked down.

Forest hated this. He wanted Ellery to be proud — to always look up. "We can help you," he insisted. "You're right. No one can force them to change their minds about you. But we can show them that whatever they think about you, we support you."

"What do you want me to do?"

"Face them." The plan was already forming in Forest's mind, and he hoped Ellery would help. "I want to call a meeting. I think I've spoken to all the pride members, so it's about time anyway. Gal and I will talk about the next steps we'll be taking and the problems arising. I want to include this. I want you to talk to them, to at least try to make them see what they're missing."

"I don't want to antagonize the pride. They're my family, even though it's a shitty one."

"What kind of family are they? They push you away. They insult you. They make you feel like you don't have a place here when it's not the truth." Forest sighed and took a bite of the sandwich before going on. "But I understand where you're coming from. It's terrifying to face your family and tell them what you think about them and that they've been hurting you." Forest knew better than most about that situation. It was the only reason he hadn't stood up to his parents, after all.

He didn't want to hurt them, but he also didn't want to anger them. So far, the situation back home was going okay, but eventually, Forest would have to face the fact that he needed to tell his parents the truth—that he wouldn't marry Marissa and that he'd met his mate, a man who wasn't even part of their pack.

So yes, he understood where Ellery was coming from. But if Ellery had the courage to stand up to the pride and tell them what he thought about them, then maybe Forest would have that same courage. It was ridiculous, but Forest was already so proud of Ellery for the way he was reacting to this. Instead of lashing out and pushing people away, he was staying as far as he could from them and trying to keep the peace. It was a good thing with everything that had happened to the pride, but things needed to change now that Gal and Forest were both here and at the pride was finally settling down.

"It's not just that you should stand up for yourself," Forest said. "I understand why you don't want to, and I wouldn't push if this weren't important. But it's also the fact that neither Gal nor I want to guide a pride that is this *mean*. We've never liked bullies, and we want the pride to be safe for all its members, including you." Especially him. Ellery was strong, much stronger than he gave himself credit for, and Forest hated seeing him so down. He wanted to help, but he didn't know how, except for this.

He cleared his throat. "Even if you don't want to do this, Gal has to. He won't stand for a pride that's unsafe, and right now, it is. They're bullying you, and you're an adult. What will happen if one of the children grows up to be someone they don't like and they do the same to him or her?"

It took Ellery a moment to answer, and Forest didn't rush

him. He wanted Ellery to have time to think about this, to make his decision without being pushed into it.

"I never thought about it that way," Ellery finally said.

"I know. That's one of the reasons I'm good at my job. I can see several angles in the same situation, and I put them together and show people what's going on."

"I already know what's going on. But you're right. I couldn't forgive myself if this happened to someone else and I could have done something to stop it." Ellery snatched another tomato, but he didn't eat it. "But I don't even know what they have against me."

"Anne said something about you being a traitor."

Ellery grimaced. "I guess. I mean, I wasn't surprised when people suspected me after what my father did. I got it. I still do. What I don't understand is why they still think I had something to do with all that. Liam and Gal are my friends. They always make a point of spending time with me, especially when the entire pride is gathered, like at meals. Surely they have to know that Gal and Liam wouldn't be my friends if I'd had anything to do with what happened? I mean, if I'd helped my father, I would be in the cell next to his in the council jail right now."

Forest didn't have an answer. Sometimes people acted without thinking, and he suspected that was the case here. Like Ellery, he wasn't surprised when Ellery had been suspected in the beginning. It made sense. But since it was obvious he had nothing to do with it, it was surprising that the pride didn't understand that, too.

Or maybe they did. Maybe some of the pride members stayed away because they didn't want to be involved. Forest wasn't blind. There was a reason he'd spoken to every single pride member, and it was so that he could learn the dynamics between them. He knew who had a strong personality and who would rather stay in the background. He knew who took over when groups were formed. He knew who the leaders where, who could create problems for Gal and him, and of course, Liam.

So he wasn't surprised that Anne was right smack in the middle of what was happening to Ellery. He doubted she believed Ellery had plotted with his father, but she was using this as an excuse to ostracize him, and people were following her lead because of her strong personality. She wasn't the alpha, but she might have been if she hadn't been problematic. Forest suspected she was jealous. After everything that had happened, after what Ellery's father had done, Ellery was still Liam's friend. He was Liam's *best* friend, and that had a certain weight. Anne probably thought that if Ellery wasn't there, she might be able to get closer to the alpha and the alpha mate, but that showed just how wrong she was. She thought they would abandon Ellery, that they would push him away.

That wouldn't happen, though. Ellery had done nothing wrong, and even though Forest didn't know Liam well, he knew Gal. Gal always stood for what was right, even if it created problems for him or for the group he was leading at the moment. This case was especially important since Gal was staying. This was his home now, his family, and he wouldn't allow this kind of behavior. That was the crux of the situation, and Forest wanted to get to the bottom of it. Ellery deserved more than what the pride was giving him, and Forest would make sure they knew they were behaving like assholes and that it wouldn't be allowed anymore.

Because what Anne thought didn't matter. She was just another pride member, and people shouldn't be looking to her for leadership. They should be looking at Gal, Liam, and Forest, and Forest would make sure they knew that they could.

"Thank you," Ellery murmured.

"What are you thanking me for?"

"You made me realize I wasn't alone. I needed that. I might not be crazy about your plan, but I know it's a good one."

Forest grinned at Ellery and reached for him, moving slowly enough that Ellery could move back if he wanted to.

He didn't. Instead, he let Forest hook a hand behind his neck and pull him closer, then press their lips together. Forest didn't push for more because they were both eating, but this felt good, so much so that he couldn't wait to see what happened when they kissed for real.

It would happen eventually. He knew it would. In the meantime, he would make sure Ellery knew he was there for him, whatever happened.

Chapter Four

Ellery dug his hands into the earth, enjoying the feeling of it between his fingers. He made a small hole, then settled the tiny plant into it.

He liked doing this, and he'd missed it. He'd avoided spending time in the garden because he hadn't wanted to be confronted by anyone. Anne was the leader, but even though she was in charge of the kitchen, it didn't mean she didn't influence people. The pride members taking care of the vegetable patch were closely linked to the cooks, and Ellery had felt it was better to avoid all of them.

Things were different now, though, or they should be anyway. Gal and Forest had held a pride meeting. They'd explained what had already been done, especially when it came to the house, and what they were planning next. Ellery had been impressed. He could see the house changing almost day by day, problems that had been obvious disappearing. Gal was working with the people in town and the nearby shifter groups in a way Alpha Carter never had, and the pride was flourishing as a result.

Gal and Forest had also pointed out several problems they'd found. One of them had been bullying. They hadn't mentioned Ellery's name, and Ellery was grateful for that. Still, it was obvious to everyone that they'd been talking about him, and he had to deal with a lot of hateful glares these days. He didn't care, though. Gal and Forest had stood up for him, which was more than most pride members could say. The only other people who hadn't pushed Ellery down were Liam and Helga, and although Ellery didn't mind spending time with them, he was happy to be able to do more. He wasn't hiding on his bench or in his bedroom anymore. Instead, he was doing what he enjoyed, and it was a relief.

He should have known his peace wouldn't last for long.

He heard footsteps coming behind him, and he steeled himself because he already knew what was about to happen. He'd been expecting this since the meeting, and he was surprised Anne had waited so long. He tensed when the footsteps came closer, but he didn't turn to face whoever was about to yell at him.

"What are you doing here?" Anne asked.

Ellery took a deep breath. "I thought it was obvious. I'm planting."

"You're touching food we're supposed to eat. None of us want to eat anything you've planted or gathered."

Ellery wouldn't avoid this, would he? He sighed heavily and got to his feet. He didn't want to face Anne at a disadvantage. He was already shorter than her, something he wasn't happy to realize. He turned to face her and crossed his arms over his chest. "What are you saying?"

"What do you think I'm saying? I wouldn't want to be *contaminated* by you."

Ellery wanted to run away. It was always his first instinct, and he had to fight hard against it. It wouldn't do him any good. It never had. That was the wrong way to solve the situation, but eventually, he would have to face Anne and her friends. It might as well be now.

Forest was right. Even though he and Gal had talked to the pride, even though they'd warned them of what would happen if they continued with the bullying, it hadn't helped. Anne thought she was immune to their authority, and she wouldn't stop until Ellery stood up to her, and maybe not even then. But Ellery wouldn't find out if he didn't try, and he'd had enough of scurrying in fear.

The pride was his, too. This house was his home, and he deserved to be in the garden, in the kitchen, or anywhere that wasn't a private space.

He swallowed and forced himself to say, "I don't see why you have to fear me contaminating anything. I'm not sick."

Anne snorted and looked at her friends. They stood behind her, but they didn't look as convinced as she was. "You're not sick? It runs in the family. Your father went crazy and tried to kill the alpha, and you will, too. Nothing you tell me will make me change my mind that you had something to do with it. You're planning something, aren't you? That's why you befriended Liam."

"I befriended Liam because he was nice, and we're the same age, and we get along. We've been friends for years, even though you didn't notice. Of course, you didn't notice Liam at all until he became the alpha mate, did you?"

Anne jerked back as if Ellery had slapped her. "How dare you talk to me like that?"

Ellery stood tall, or as tall as he could, anyway. "How dare *you* insinuate that I had anything to do with what my father did? I didn't. I would never hurt anyone, least of all Liam and his mate. He's my friend, and so is Gal. You have no proof that I helped my father, and you know why that is? Because I *didn't.*"

"No one believes you," she spat out.

"I don't care if you believe me or not. I don't care if any of you believe me. But I won't let you bully me anymore. We're adults, and we should act like adults. Instead, you're behaving like a third-grade little girl who's afraid I'm going to take something from her. Why are you afraid of me, Anne? What do you think I will do to you?"

Ellery took a step closer to her, and to his surprise, she stepped back. She bumped into her friends, and they scattered, leaving Ellery and Anne facing each other.

Ellery hadn't expected that, and he wasn't sure what to do. He decided to push his luck and tell Anne everything he hadn't told her over the past few months.

"I don't know what you have in mind," he began. "I don't know if you think you can manipulate Liam if I'm not here anymore, or if you think you'll become his friend instead of me. I don't know, and I don't care. Liam isn't stupid, and he sees right through you. He might be the only one, but I don't care about anyone else. You should have been my family, especially after what happened with my father, but instead, you pushed me away. You want me to fail. You want me to leave the pride, and while I don't know why, I'm not going to do it. I won't give you the satisfaction. This is my home just as much as it is yours. I've always been a good pride member. I've always done what was asked of me, and I never complained. You have a problem with me, that's fine. If you don't want to solve it by talking to me, that's fine, too. But stop this. Stop bullying me and whoever else you're doing this to. No one here deserves that."

"I haven't done anything. I'm not a bully. I just want people to know the truth."

Ellery threw his hands in the air. She didn't understand, did she? Or maybe she did, and she didn't care. "What did I ever do to you?" Because there had to be a good reason. Ellery didn't want to think Anne was a bad person, but he didn't understand her or her behavior.

"It's not fair."

Ellery blinked. "What's not fair?"

Anne pointed a finger at him. He had to resist the urge to take a step back. He didn't want to show her he was afraid, and honestly, now that she was alone, he wasn't. Even if she shifted into her tiger form and attacked him, he knew he could take her on, at least for a few moments. Then someone would notice what was happening and would come to separate them.

"It's not fair," she repeated. "You influence the alpha mate. You shouldn't. You're no one. I've been working my ass off for the pride for so many years, and instead of being held to my rightful position, instead of making me the beta or at the very least listening to what I have to say, the alpha mate is always with you."

Ellery frowned. He might be biased, but Anne would be a terrible beta. Her behavior toward him was a clear indication of that. He wasn't about to tell her that, though, so he focused on the second part. "So? It's because we're friends. It has nothing to do with the pride."

"You're going to use him. You're going to use your influence on him to kick me and others out. You only want the men here. You don't like women, and we all know that."

Ellery laughed. He couldn't help it, not after what Anne had just said. "And you think what? That I want the pride to be made up only of guys? I might be gay, but I have no intention of sleeping with anyone. Trust me, none of the pride members are my type." He paused, wondering if maybe she wasn't saying everything. It didn't make much sense to him, but what did he know? He wasn't in her head. "Neither is your husband, so you don't have to worry about me trying to steal him from you."

She huffed and raised her shoulders, but now that Ellery thought he understood what was behind her hatred, she didn't scare him anymore. She shouldn't have scared him to begin with, but he'd let his emotions take over, and this was the result.

"You won't take my husband away from me because I forbid you to get anywhere near him."

"I wasn't planning to." Her husband was a nice man, but even if he wasn't married, he wouldn't be Ellery's type. No,

Ellery's type tended to redheads who laughed a lot and were sweet and took care of him. Ellery's type was his mate, and maybe it was time to do something about that.

Ellery had let fear rule his life until now, but enough was enough. He needed to start living, and he would only be able to do that if he let go of the fear and took a leap of faith.

That was exactly what he needed to do with it when it came to Forest in a relationship.

Forest was so fucking proud of Ellery. He'd heard everything through the open window of his office, and he'd made sure not to make noise so Ellery wouldn't notice him. He wanted to go out there, tear Anne a new one and tell her that she needed to talk to Gal because this wouldn't be tolerated, but instead, he stayed right where he was. It was something Ellery had to do on his own, and he was.

Still, he took notes of who was bullying Ellery. He'd already known about Anne because she was one of the pushy ones. He hadn't realized why until now, and he still didn't, not quite. He wrote down the names of the other people who'd been with her, even though they hadn't said anything to Ellery. They were there for support. As far as Forest was concerned, they were just as guilty as Anne. This had been going on for too long, and Ellery didn't deserve any of it.

Forest would investigate further, but from what he'd just heard, he suspected Ellery was right. She'd thought that she could have an in with Gal, but instead, Ellery did. He would never use it for his own gain, but Anne couldn't see that. She was too busy hating Ellery and making his life hard to realize that. Not that it mattered. What *did* matter was the way she acted, and Forest wouldn't forget that.

Once he was done writing down all the names he could remember, he leaned out the window. Ellery was facing him, and he jerked back, obviously surprised. Forest grinned at him. "Ellery. Do you mind coming to my office for a moment?"

Anne twirled around at the sound of Forest's voice. She smiled, looking like the cat who ate the canary. She probably thought Forest was going to berate Ellery for what he'd said. He would never berate his mate for standing up for himself. Hell, he'd been pushing Ellery to do just that.

"You heard what she said to me," Ellery said.

"I heard the entire conversation," Forest confirmed.

Anne paled, but she was quick to gather herself. "He's lying. He can't know what I feel or think."

"The same goes for you, doesn't it? You don't know what he thinks or feels, so why do you hate him?"

Forest didn't wait for her to give him an answer. He didn't care. Her kind of people didn't need a reason to bully people. They took pleasure in it. Ellery wouldn't be happy to have Forest step in, but it was Forest's job. He was the beta, and he was the one who kept the peace in the pride.

He waved at Ellery to come to the office and waited until Ellery had finally stepped away from Anne to lean back into the room. He settled behind his desk, waiting for his mate to arrive. Ellery was smiling when he stepped into the office and closed the door behind himself. "Were you spying on me?" he asked.

Forest couldn't help but smile. "Of course not. It's not my fault that my office gives onto the garden and that you and Anne decided to fight this out just under it."

"We weren't fighting."

"I don't know. It sure sounded like it." He wanted to protect his mate, but maybe Ellery didn't need him to. He'd held his own just fine with Anne, and hopefully, he would continue to do so. Forest wouldn't always be there to listen to their conversation, and Forest hoped Ellery wouldn't need him to be.

He pushed away from his desk and patted his knees. "Why don't you come here?"

Ellery's cheeks flushed, but he still stepped closer to the desk. "Where do you want me to sit?"

"In my lap."

"Are you sure? Someone could see us from the window. I'm pretty sure Anne is still there, bitching to her friends about how I dared to talk to her."

"And I should care, why? You're my mate, Ellery." Forest softened his voice. "I'm not going to hide that from anyone. I haven't told people because I wasn't sure whether or not you wanted me to, but that doesn't change the fact that I won't put you to the side. You're my mate. You're important to me, and I want everyone to know that."

Ellery sighed and finally came closer. Forest allowed him to move however he wanted, and he wouldn't have protested if Ellery had decided to sit on the other side of the desk instead of in Forest's lap. Still, he was relieved when Ellery settled on his thighs.

Ellery was tense, as if he wasn't used to this, and Forest suspected that was the case. No one had been allowed to date outside the pride. He didn't know if Ellery had ex-boyfriends, but he was sheltered in a way Forest wasn't used to. Forest knew nothing would happen between them if he didn't take the first step, so he cupped Ellery's cheek and pulled his face closer, kissing him.

They'd been kissing more frequently since the first kiss they shared on the bench outside, but that was where things always stopped. Forest never wanted to push Ellery too far, and he felt unusually hesitant when he was with his mate. He didn't know if it was because of what Ellery had been through or because of the bond they shared, and he didn't think it mattered. He wanted to take his time with his mate — to make sure things were as perfect as they could be. Both of them were human beings, so of course, nothing would ever be a hundred percent perfect, but Forest could strive for the next best thing.

He stroked a hand down Ellery's side, then decided to push a bit and slipped it under Ellery's t-shirt. His skin was warm and he smelled of earth and the outside, with a hint of sweat under it. It was delicious, and it made Forest want to eat him up.

Ellery blushed even harder, but to Forest's surprise, Ellery didn't push him away. Instead, he wrapped his arms around him and pulled himself close, making Forest wish they weren't in a chair, but rather, in a bed. Hell, he would have made do with a couch. There was nothing of the kind in the office, though, so he helped Ellery straddle him rather than being seated sideways on his thighs.

"What are we doing?" Ellery asked in a whisper. He sounded breathless, and Forest felt smug that he'd been the one to do that.

"I thought it was obvious. We're making out."

"You want more?" Ellery's voice was hesitant.

Forest wasn't sure how to answer that. He decided to go with the truth. "I always want more when it comes to you, but this is fine, too."

Ellery shook his head. "You should get what you want."

"I'm sure I will eventually, but we never talked about our experiences and what we want. We should probably do that before doing more."

Ellery's eyes narrowed. "What if I don't want to wait? What if I'm done being cautious and afraid? I know you won't hurt me. You're the perfect person to take a risk with."

Forest was humbled that Ellery thought that about him. "I'm not going to protest if you want to do more than kissing. I want you, Ellery. If I had my way, you'd be in my bed every night, and I would wake up next to you every morning. But I know we need to take things slow."

Ellery thrust his hips against Forest. He was hard in his jeans, and Forest wanted to touch him. He wanted to get Ellery naked under him, but he knew this wasn't the right place or moment. Still, that didn't mean they couldn't push things a bit. The door was closed, and as long as they stayed quiet, no one would know what was happening.

He slipped a hand between them, swiftly opened Ellery's jeans, and pushed his hand inside. Ellery wriggled, biting his lower lip as if not to cry out.

Forest leaned closer. "Good mate. Don't make too much noise or someone will come. Or do you want that to happen?"

Ellery shook his head frantically. "No. This is only for us."

"I agree. That means you can't make any noise. Understood?"

Ellery nodded, and Forest focused on him. His cock was slender and proportionate to his body. It would be perfect in Forest's mouth or in his ass, but he had to make do with having it in his hand. It was better than nothing, and he made sure to touch every single inch of it, indulging himself. He spread the moisture beading at the head and jacked it off, enjoying how Ellery squirmed on top of him. He wanted more. He suspected he would always want more with Ellery, but for now, this was good.

Ellery wriggled harder, but to Forest's surprise, he managed not to make any kind of noise. He was biting his lower lip so hard that Forest wouldn't have been surprised if he'd drawn blood, but when Ellery finally came, throwing his head back and groaning, Forest saw that he hadn't broken the skin. He leaned closer and sucked on the poor lip, trying to soothe the sting Ellery had to feel.

He looked down between them when Ellery slumped against him. "That was nice, but now I need to clean up and probably change my shirt."

Ellery blushed. "I'm sorry."

"Don't be. I loved doing this with you."

"You didn't come," Ellery quietly said, working his hand down Forest's chest.

Forest clutched Ellery's hips. "Not yet."

His phone rang.

Forest swore, but he couldn't ignore it. It might be important. He snatched it from the desk and answered without looking at it. "Hello?"

"Forest?"

Forest blinked. "Dad?"

"You have to come home, son. Your mother had a heart attack."

Ellery knew something was wrong right away. Forest paled, and Ellery held his breath, listening in to the conversation.

"Heart attack?" he asked.

Ellery could hear the whisper of the man on the other side of the phone. "She's okay. But I need you to come home, please."

Ellery didn't know what to do. He wanted to comfort Forest, but he'd been in his shoes once, and he knew that nothing he could do or say would help him feel better.

Ellery had lost his mom to illness, and even though years had passed, he still mourned her. He would never tell Forest that everything would be okay because neither of them could know it would be, but he snuggled closer, wrapping himself around his mate and hoping that his presence would help at least a bit.

"Of course I'll come home," Forest said. "It'll take a bit, but I'll be there soon as I can."

"That's all I'm asking for. And don't rush. I don't want you to get into an accident. The doctors are positive that she'll be fine."

It wasn't enough. Ellery could see it in Forest's expression. He was terrified for his mother, and Ellery understood that better than most people. He stayed right where he was even after Forest hung up, pressed against him, wishing there was more he could do.

Forest wrapped his arms around Ellery and held him close. He wasn't crying, but he was still pale, and he looked like he wanted to bolt.

Ellery wiggled to get off Forest lap. "Find Gal. He has to know about this. Do you need me to do anything?" Ellery could pack Forest a bag or maybe some food for the trip. He didn't know where Forest was headed, but he would do everything he could to make his mate feel better. Not good, because that wouldn't happen until Forest saw his mother, but okay.

Forest blinked and looked at Ellery. "I want you to come with me."

Ellery sucked in a breath. "Come with you? You mean to see your mother?"

Forest nodded and took one of Ellery's hands. "Please. I can't do this on my own."

"Of course you can." It didn't sound like a good idea. Actually, it sounded like a pretty bad idea. Ellery knew Forest hadn't told anyone but Gal that they were mates. That included his parents, and now would be the worst time to tell them about him.

"I need you there. I know we haven't talked about this or anything, really, and if you don't want me to, I won't tell anyone we're mates. But please. I can't go there on my own."

Ellery couldn't say no. Forest was in need, and he needed *him*. That had never happened before. No one had never needed Ellery, and while Ellery felt a little lost as to what to do, he didn't want to let Forest down. "I'll come." He wanted to give his mate everything he needed, even though he didn't know what it was yet.

Forest's shoulders slumped, and he looked relieved. "Thank you." He rubbed his face. "I don't know what to do. I hate feeling this way."

Ellery got to his feet and pulled Forest out of his chair. He straightened Forest's clothes, then guided him toward the door. "The first thing you need to do is talk to Gal. Tell him what's happening and that you need some time off. Once that's done, we'll go to your room and pack some of your stuff. Are we driving there, or do I need to buy plane tickets? Or maybe contact a Nix?"

Forest shook his head. "Driving. I don't want to shimmer there and be stuck without a vehicle. It'll take us several hours, but I don't think I can be on a plane right now."

Ellery was relieved. He'd never been further than Green Hill. He would have done it for Forest, of course, but he felt better at the thought that he would be in a car rather than in a box shooting through the sky.

"I'll pack some food, too," he said.

Forest hesitated. "I can do that part."

Ellery knew he was thinking about Anne and her friends, but for once, they didn't scare Ellery. He had to do this for Forest, and it was easy to forget how terrifying it usually was. Maybe it was because Forest needed him, or maybe because he'd finally faced Anne. Ellery didn't know, and it didn't matter.

"I can do it, don't worry. Go find Gal. I'll go to the kitchen. Then we can meet upstairs and go to our rooms to pack. Okay? Or do you want me to come with you to Gal?" Ellery would do it, but the sooner they got out of the house, the better it would be.

Forest shook his head. "I can do it. But thank you." He hesitated. "I know you probably don't want anything to do with my family right now, but I don't know if I can do this without you."

"Don't worry about me. Anything you need, you tell me, and I'll do my best to give it to you. Okay?"

"I don't want you to feel obligated to come with me if you don't want to."

"It's *fine*. I can't say I'm crazy about it, mostly because I don't think you've told your parents about me and it's going to be awkward, but it's fine. I promise. Being away from the pride will probably be good for me, even though I've never traveled."

Forest's eyes widened. "I'd forgotten about that. Are you sure you feel up to coming with me?"

Ellery kissed Forest's cheek. "I'm sure. Come on. We both have stuff to do. Stop worrying about me and focus on what you need to do so we can leave."

Forest nodded. He still looked a little lost, but it was better than before, and Ellery had a hard time believing that just telling Forest he would be there could do that, that it reassured him and made him feel better.

Forest finally left to talk to the alpha, and Ellery rushed to the kitchen. Anne wasn't there, thankfully, but her friends were, and they glared at Ellery. They didn't say anything, though, and Ellery did his best to ignore them. Forest needed him, and it made him braver. He wasn't sure he liked it—he should be brave on his own, not because of someone else—but it didn't matter. What he was doing did, though, and he opened the fridge, grabbing enough to make several sandwiches. He packed them into a bag, then added fruit and vegetables that would keep for several hours. He didn't know where they were going, but Forest had said it would be several hours of driving, and even though he probably wouldn't be hungry, Ellery would make sure he ate.

Ellery also packed a few bottles of water, then headed out

of the kitchen. He almost collided with Liam, who was walking in.

Liam grabbed Ellery's shoulders to steady him and grabbed one of the bottles of water that almost fell to the floor. "Everything okay?" he asked.

Ellery shrugged. "I'm fine. Forest, on the other hand, isn't."

"I saw him in Gal's office. He told us about his mom and that you were going with him to visit her." Liam hesitated. Ellery wished he hadn't, because he needed to go, but he waited for his best friend to speak his mind. "Are you sure it's a good idea? I understand that you want to be with him and to support him, but things haven't gone very far between the two of you, have they? Are you sure you're up to meeting his family?"

"I don't think I'll ever be up to meeting his family, but I have to do this. I promise I'll be careful."

"Oh, that's not that I'm worried about. But you don't know anything about Forest's family, and you don't know how they'll react. If you need anything, and I mean *anything*, call me. Gal and I can be with you in a few hours, or we can even contact a Nix and have them shimmer us to you. Understood?"

Ellery's heart swelled in his chest. He wasn't as alone as he'd thought he was. Liam would be there for him, no matter what.

He didn't know what would happen with Forest's family, but he was ready to face this. He knew that if he needed to come home, he wouldn't be alone, and that made all the difference.

Forest had known Gal wouldn't have a problem with him leaving, but he was still relieved when Gal pushed him toward the door of his office. "Of course you can go. Why did you even ask?"

Forest stopped. He didn't want to do this in the hallway where anyone could hear them. "I just wanted to be sure. I just arrived, and I haven't done a lot. I'm so sorry to leave so soon."

"Don't even mention it. We're talking about your mother. I can hold down the fort. Don't worry about the pride or me. It won't be a problem. Just let me know if you're not coming back, okay?"

Forest blinked. "What do you mean?"

Gal rubbed the back of his neck. "You know. If you plan to stay with your family, I'll understand, of course. But I need to know so I can request another beta."

Forest crossed his arms over his chest and glared at Gal. He knew he needed to go, but this couldn't wait. "Why would you think I might stay there? I never mentioned anything like that." That would be because Forest had no intention of staying home. He called it home, but it really wasn't, not anymore. It hadn't been in years, and even though he wanted to see his parents and make sure his mother was okay, he had every intention of coming back.

Green Hill wasn't home, either, but it could be. He'd given it some thought after meeting Ellery, and he found that it didn't scare him anymore. He'd been moving around for years, never stopping more than a few months at a time, but he knew he couldn't do that anymore. Ellery was more important, and Green Hill wasn't a bad place to stay. Gal was here, and so was Liam, whom Forest liked. The pride wasn't perfect by any means, but most of the members were good people. Forest could see himself staying here, maybe building a family. He'd never thought about having kids, but meeting Ellery had made him realize everything he would miss out on if he continued traveling.

He hadn't made a decision yet, but he was leaning toward

staying, and he was surprised at himself.

"I promise, I'm not leaving forever," he told Gal. "I do need to be with my family, but it won't be for long."

Gal shook his head. "Take all the time you need. And like I said, I'll understand if you decide to stay. I just need to know."

"Goddammit, Gal. I'm not planning to stay. You know what would happen if I did. I have no intention of marrying Marissa, and I know my parents are going to push for that to happen."

Forest loved his parents. He hated that his mother was in pain and that she'd had a heart attack. It wasn't common in shifters, but it happened. He also knew her, though. If she was okay, if she could talk, she would ask him to come back. She'd wanted it for years, and now she had a perfect reason. She could use her health to lure Forest back to the family, and maybe even to push him into this marriage. She didn't know about Ellery, and that was Forest's fault.

He'd been planning to tell his parents about Ellery, of course. He hadn't known how, and he'd pushed the revelation back, promising himself that eventually, he would tell them. Now wasn't the perfect moment by any means, but it was a moment that would have to do. Forest needed to deal with this. He couldn't allow his parents to steamroll him and push him around, no matter how much he loved them.

"Ellery is coming with me," he told Gal.

Gal's eyes widened. "He is? Are you sure it's a good idea?"

"I don't know if it is, but I need him."

"You should probably tell him what your parents are planning. He'll want to know, especially once he's face-to-face with them."

He was right, and Forest wasn't looking forward to that conversation. "I'll make sure he knows." Because it wouldn't be right for Ellery to face Forest's parents while not knowing that they'd been planning the rest of his life since he was a kid.

They wanted Forest to marry the alpha's daughter. They wanted him to settle down back home, and eventually, to become the next alpha. There was nothing that terrified Forest more than having to take on that role, though. He didn't know how Gal did it, but he was more than happy being a beta. Hell, some days, the responsibilities that came with the beta role were almost too much for him. He couldn't imagine what being an alpha would be like.

Gal squeezed Forest's shoulder. "I'll wait to hear from you, then," he said. "Not because you might decide to stay there," he added in a rush before Forest could scold him again. "I got the message. You're not going anywhere long term. I'm relieved. The pride is settling down, but I know I'm not as close to the members as I should be."

Forest clapped Gal's back. "I shouldn't be longer than a week." Because Forest had a life to come back to. Also, from what his father had said, while his mother was in the hospital, she wasn't anywhere near dying, and it was a relief. Forest would stay there for as long as he could, but that was their life, and this was his.

He hoped they suspected he didn't want to marry Marissa or stay with them. It would be less of a shock for them if they did. Surely they'd thought about why he never came home and why he'd taken this job. And if they hadn't, well, he would have to tell them. He wasn't about to hide who Ellery was to him. He never wanted to treat Ellery badly, not after what he'd gone through. He was proud to call Ellery his mate, and he couldn't wait to see what would happen next in their relationship. He'd have to make sure his parents didn't ruin everything. He'd need to talk to Ellery, and while he wasn't looking forward to that conversation, he knew Ellery would understand.

Ellery had a strong sense of loyalty to the pride, even though the pride didn't deserve it. He would understand why Forest hadn't talked to his parents yet. Forest needed his mate with him, and he couldn't afford to fight with Ellery while they headed to see his parents. He would have to focus on his mother and to talk to the alpha. The man had agreed to have his daughter marry Forest eventually, but Forest knew that he would understand, too.

Or at least, he hoped so.

The alpha had always looked at Forest like a son, so it would be hard, but he wasn't a bad man. Forest would have to deal with all of this much sooner than he'd thought and planned. He was ready, though.

There was no backing off from it. He'd met Ellery, and he wasn't going to hide him. This was just a snag in the plan, and hopefully, the trip would bring them closer than they were already. It would give them time to talk. Forest was worried about his mother, and he couldn't wait to see her, but he knew there was no way he'd be able to stay silent the entire time it took for him and Ellery to get there. He talked when he was nervous, and today wasn't any different. If anything, he was even more nervous than usual. He was worried about his mother.

"Now go," Gal said, pushing Forest toward the door.

"Promise me you'll call me if you have a problem? And I mean anything. I can deal with whatever the pride throws your way, but I need to know about it."

Gal laughed. "I love you, Forest, but I can take care of this on my own. I'm not entirely useless."

Forest flushed. "I never said you were useless. But like you said, you're not as close to the pride as you could be. Not that I'm blaming you for that. You've had other things to focus on until now. But if you need anything at all, call me. I can answer whatever question you have about the pride members."

"I'll do that, but you need to focus on your mother. She's the most important thing right now. Let me know how she is."

Forest nodded and finally left. He wasn't looking forward to the trip, but he knew that everything would be okay once he came back. He had a home now, and a mate. It was everything he hadn't thought he needed, but now that he had them, he couldn't do without them.

CHAPTER FIVE

Forest seemed to know exactly where to go when they arrived at the hospital, so Ellery followed him without a word. The tension in the car had been high the entire time, and Forest talked for just as long. Ellery hadn't realized he was the kind of person who babbled when they were stressed, but he definitely was. It was adorable, and Ellery would have teased him in another situation. This wasn't the kind of situation he wanted to tease his mate about, though.

"Have you heard from your father?" he asked as they exited the elevator.

"He texted me the floor and the room number." Forest didn't even look at Ellery, but Ellery didn't blame him. He could deal without his mate's attention for a bit, especially when Forest's mother was having health trouble. Hopefully, she was okay.

Forest finally slowed down once they'd gone about halfway down the hallway. Two men stood outside a room, quietly talking, and they both looked up when they heard Forest and Ellery's footsteps. One of the men took a step back, while the other rushed toward Forest. He opened his arms, and Forest wrapped himself around him. That was all Ellery needed to know that this was Forest's father.

"You were quicker than I thought," Forest's father said. Ellery wished he'd asked Forest what his parents' names were, but he hadn't wanted to remind him why they were coming while he was driving.

"I promise I didn't go over the speed limits. I *can't* promise

I wasn't close, though."

Forest's father laughed, but the sound wasn't entirely happy. He took a step back and held his son at arm's length, looking him up and down. "You look good. Better than expected."

Forest scowled at him. "What did you think? That Gal wasn't feeding me? You know him. You've *met* him. You know what kind of man and alpha he is."

Forest's father shook his head. "I know the kind of alpha he is, but that doesn't mean I trust him with my son."

Forest took a step back. "How is Mom? What did the doctor say?"

"She's okay, don't worry. It was a heart attack, but the doctors say that with a change in diet and less stress, she'll be perfectly fine, and she'll live long enough to meet her grandchildren."

"Dad," Forest said with a groan.

His father ignored him. "Marissa was just here, but she had to leave. I'm sure she'll be happy to meet you later, though. She said she'd be back as soon as she could. She can't wait to see you."

Ellery frowned. He didn't know who Marissa was, and Forest hadn't mentioned any sisters or cousins. She might have been a family friend, of course, but something in the way Forest's father said her name made Ellery feel uneasy. Forest's grimace at the mention of her also didn't help.

"Can we not talk about this right now?" Forest asked. "I want to see Mom."

"The nurse is with her right now. You can see her later. But we need to talk, Forest."

"Not now, Dad. Please."

Forest stepped around his father and reached for the door, but his father stopped him with a hand on his chest. "No. Not later. Your mother and I have waited long enough. It's time,

Forest."

Forest raked a hand through his hair. "No, it's not. I love you and Mom, but—"

"If you love us, you'll move back here. This is your home and your family. You should never have left, but I thought that after a while, you would see that you're better off here. What are you doing out there that's so important?"

"I'm helping people. *That's* what I'm doing."

"I'm proud of you for everything you do, but you're hurting your family, Forest. I can't stand for that. You need to realize what's going on and act accordingly."

Forest's expression tightened. "I've always realized what was going on. You and Mom want me to live my life the way you want, not the way I do. I've always known that, and it's the reason I left."

"How can you say that? We don't want you to do anything you don't want."

Forest snorted loudly. "Of course you do. I can do everything I want as long as you're okay with it. But if you don't approve, then I should forget it. You just told me I needed to come home, but you didn't even think that maybe I don't want to do that. *You* think it's the right thing to do, not me. You didn't even ask me what I want. You just—you expect me to *obey*."

Ellery looked around. He had no idea what was going on, but it was a conversation that was better kept private. He should probably leave and find some food, even though he wasn't hungry. It was obvious Forest and his father needed to speak, and they should do that with no one around to listen.

To Ellery's relief, the other man stepped closer. "Why don't the two of you wait to have this conversation?" he asked. "I'm sure Forest is tired and stressed because of what's happening to Diane, and you are, too. If you talk about this now, you might say something you don't mean and will regret."

Forest's father looked like he wanted to say no, but instead, he nodded curtly. "All right. I'll wait. But I want answers this time, Forest. You've been avoiding this conversation for too long. I should have pushed before your mother got sick."

"Are you saying it's my fault?" Forest snapped.

The other man raised his hands. "Enough of that." There was something in his tone that said that he was used to being obeyed.

Once again, Ellery wondered who he was. He still didn't know what was happening, and it made him uncomfortable. He hated feeling lost and like he didn't matter. It was as if neither of three men had noticed he was standing there, and he would have left if he'd been sure Forest wouldn't need him.

A few seconds later, he wished he'd gone when he'd been able to. The second man turned toward him. "And who is that?"

Ellery swallowed and looked at Forest. He wasn't about to say anything Forest wasn't okay with, but Ellery didn't *know* what Forest was okay with. He wanted to tell the man that he was Forest's mate, but he wasn't about to create more problems. Forest already seemed to have enough of them.

Forest rubbed the back of his neck. "This is Ellery."

"Why did you bring a friend?" Forest's father asked. "This is a family matter. Your mother isn't up for socializing."

"Why wouldn't I have brought him? And why are you complaining? You don't know him. You have no idea who he is or why he's here."

"Please," the second man said.

Ellery suspected that Forest and his father would end up yelling at each other if no one interrupted them. He took a step back, intent on going back to the car at least until things had calmed down, but the second man looked at him again. To Ellery's surprise, he offered him his hand. "I'm Alpha

Young. You can call me Steve, since you're a friend of Forest."

Ellery blinked. Of course. He should have realized that this man was Forest's alpha — or rather, his parents'. Forest hadn't been a part of his family and this pack for a while.

He shook the man's hand. "I'm Ellery."

"So Forest said. That doesn't help us understand who you are, though. Are you're a friend of his? You don't have to answer, but I'd appreciate it. I like to know who I'm talking to."

Ellery looked at Forest again. How was he supposed to answer the question? Did Forest want his father and Alpha Young to know Ellery with his mate?

Ellery had too many questions and zero answers. It would be better if he kept his mouth shut, so that was what he did. He pressed his lips together and stared at Forest, mentally asking him to answer. He was terrified of what would come out of Forest's mouth, though. He didn't know if he could stand it if Forest confirmed that they were just friends.

Forest was tired and annoyed, and he didn't want to deal with this right now. He realized he should have talked to his parents sooner. He wished he had, but it was too late now. He'd waited because he hadn't wanted to fight with them, especially when he didn't have a good reason.

He was grateful for the interruption, but he hadn't expected Alpha Young to ask what Ellery was to him. He should have. Of course the alpha would wonder who Ellery was since Forest had arrived with him, and he'd been standing there while Forest's father talked to him.

"I *am* Forest's friend," Ellery said after what felt like ages.

He'd broken the silence, and Forest didn't know what to say. Ellery wasn't his friend, or rather, he wasn't just his friend. He was so much more, and Forest hated himself for allowing Ellery to do this.

"It's not true," he said, his tone a little too harsh. He didn't want Ellery to lie. He didn't want Ellery to feel like he *had* to lie.

Alpha Young blinked at him. "I'm sorry? Is Ellery your friend, or not?"

This was hard, harder than Forest had thought. He hadn't realized how difficult it would be to tell his parents that he wasn't moving back. That was why he'd avoided the conversation in the first place. But now, he couldn't anymore.

He didn't want to hide Ellery or to lie about who he was to him. He would never do that. Still, knowing that he was breaking all the dreams his parents had for him was weird. That wouldn't stop him, though. He was doing this—finally.

He cleared his throat and looked at his father. "Ellery is my mate."

That got him the reaction he'd expected. Alpha Young's eyes widened while Forest's father jerked back as if Forest had hit him. He looked at Ellery, then back at Forest again, obviously confused, surprised, and maybe slightly angry. "What do you mean?" he asked.

"Exactly what I said. Ellery is my mate. We met recently, and I wanted him to come with me and support me."

"What are you talking about? Support you? For what?"

"Maybe this isn't the right place or moment," Alpha Young repeated. Forest agreed, but he also knew his father wouldn't let it go. He was stubborn, exactly like Forest.

His father turned to Alpha Young. "You heard him. He says that boy is his mate."

Ellery stiffened, and Forest understood. He was a man, not a boy. "I'm saying he's my mate because he is," Forest said. "And don't insult him, please. You don't even know him. You wouldn't even think about insulting a stranger normally. The fact that he's my mate doesn't give you a pass."

His father threw his hands in the air. "What does that even

mean? I didn't insult him."

"You called him a boy. And you think he's the reason I won't come home, but he's not, so leave him alone. I decided not to come back a long time ago. I just never told you."

His father opened his mouth again, but Alpha Young stepped in. "Enough. I understand you're angry, Paul, but I have to insist you wait to do this. I won't have you make a scene in the middle of the hospital. I understand why you want to speak to Forest, and you'll be able to do that as soon as we head home. In the meantime, you should focus on your wife."

Forest's father's cheeks flushed, and Forest suspected he looked pretty much the same. He wasn't ashamed, but he understood where the alpha was coming from. There were people in the hospital, in the same hallway as they were in, who could hear everything they were saying. They weren't being discrete, which was weird, because Forest's father had always been on the reserved side. Today, he didn't seem to care, maybe because of what had happened to Forest's mother.

Forest rubbed his face. He didn't like fighting with his father, but he wasn't about to back down. Alpha Young wasn't wrong, though. Forest was here for his mother, and he hadn't even seen her yet. No matter how many times his father told him she was okay, he wanted to see it with his own two eyes.

"The two of you should go in," the alpha continued. "Forest, I'm sure you want to speak to your mother. Ellery and I will wait outside. I hope the two of you won't cause a commotion."

He wasn't ordering them to do anything, but he was clear—he didn't want them to make a scene. Forest was tempted to do it anyway because he knew that right now, his father was already thinking of ways to keep him here, but he knew better. Alpha Young might not be Forest's alpha anymore, but that didn't mean he didn't have authority over him.

Forest was a beta. He found himself instinctively following the lead of alphas, maybe because it was his job, or maybe because it was ingrained in him.

It didn't matter, because Alpha Young was right — Forest needed to wait. His parents would have an opportunity to yell at him soon anyway. He might as well not let either of them do it in the middle of the hospital.

"Of course, Alpha Young," Forest's father said. He looked at Forest, and Forest held his breath.

He'd known his parents would be angry. They'd had a lot of plans for him, and all of them hinged on the fact that he would eventually come back and marry Marissa. He'd never wanted that, but even though he'd told them more than once, they hadn't believed him. They'd always thought that he would come back and do what they wanted him to do because they viewed it as his duty.

He wouldn't. Now they had the proof in front of their eyes. They couldn't deny it anymore, because Ellery was in the picture, and Forest had no intention of not having him in his life. It had to be hard for Forest's father to accept it, and Forest could probably have been nicer about it, but he'd had enough. They'd never understood when he told them that getting married to the alpha's daughter wasn't what he wanted. Now, they could see it. They wouldn't be able to ignore it anymore.

"Of course. Can we go in now?" he asked.

His father huffed. "I'll see if the nurse is done."

Forest wanted to see his mother, but he also wasn't looking forward to it. His father hadn't taken this well, but it would be even worse with her. Both of them wanted Forest to marry Marissa, but his mother had always had that future planned in her mind. She used to talk about how beautiful Forest and Marissa's babies would be, how happy they would make her. Now she would have to accept that they would never be part of her life, and Forest couldn't help but wonder if this might be too much stress for her heart.

Maybe now wasn't the right moment to come out to her like this. Perhaps he shouldn't have brought Ellery with him.

But he didn't want to lie about Ellery. Ellery was his mate, his future, and considering everything that was happening, Forest doubted there would be a better moment than this one to tell his parents about him and what he was planning to do with his life.

At least his mother was already in the hospital. If something happened, someone would be there to help her right away.

It could be much, much worse, and Forest hoped he wasn't about to find out *how* much worse things could be.

Ellery watched Forest disappear into the room with his father. He only relaxed once the door closed behind them.

That could have gone better. It could have gone so, *so* much better, and he wasn't quite sure what to do now.

"So, Ellery. I have to say this was a surprise," Alpha Young said.

Ellery didn't know the guy, and he didn't trust him, but he was an alpha, and they were alone. "I don't think anyone expected this."

The alpha laughed. "You're right. What do you say if we go downstairs to grab a coffee? We can give Forest and his father some time with Diane. It's going to be a while. She was awake when I saw her earlier, and I'm sure she'll have some choice words for Forest."

Ellery rubbed the back of his neck. He wanted answers, and Forest wasn't going to give them to him since he wasn't there. It didn't feel right to ask someone else, but Ellery was curious, and he needed to know before he put more of his heart in his relationship with Forest. "Sure. We can go get coffee."

The alpha smiled. "Good."

Ellery was silent as they walked away. He didn't know how to begin, and he didn't want to sound rude. He knew he would, though. He needed to know that Forest wasn't jerking him around and having fun at his expense.

"There's a tradition for us," the alpha suddenly said. "We organize marriages."

Ellery blinked. "I'm sorry?"

"You know. Parents arrange marriages, and usually, things go well. I know it's archaic, but it works for us. I don't do anything to enforce the marriages, though. Everyone is free to choose who they want to marry, but usually, they do follow their parents' choices."

Ellery sucked in a breath. "And Forest was supposed to marry Marissa." Whoever that was. *Dammit.* Why hadn't Forest told Ellery about this? It should be the first thing to tell your mate when you met him. It would only have taken a few words, like, *hi, I'm your mate, but I'm supposed to marry someone else because my parents want me to.*

"I always suspected that Forest wouldn't marry my daughter," Alpha Young continued.

The hole in Ellery's stomach became a pit. "Your daughter?"

"Marissa. She's my daughter, and she and Forest were childhood friends. I always thought Forest wasn't crazy about the idea of marrying her. It's a pity, because he's a good man, and he would be good for our pack, even though he's only ever been a beta."

"Right. Because you're the alpha, and whoever marries your daughter could potentially become the next alpha once you retire."

"Exactly. I was happy because Forest has a lot of experience with other shifter groups. I thought that made him perfect for taking my place once I decide to step down. I know he had reservations, though. He's a beta, and being an alpha is very different. But he's never said anything, and I always went along with it."

"What do *you* think about it?" That was probably not the smartest question, but Ellery needed a few seconds to wrap his mind around everything he'd just learned.

"I would have been happy if Forest had married Marissa. But I'm okay with him not doing it. He was never eager, and I don't think my daughter is, either. It might have sounded romantic when they were younger, but they're not anymore." He chuckled. "Or rather, they're not *as* young anymore. Forest has you, and I'm sure that my daughter will find someone else, maybe someone of her own choosing. I think the only reason she hasn't told me about it yet is that it's tradition."

"And you won't force them to get married?"

Ellery was relieved when Alpha Young looked amused rather than angry. "Of course not. I won't force anyone to get married. Marriage is a personal choice. While it's true that most of the arranged marriages in our pack work, not all of them do, and not all of them involve love. Forest's parents were lucky because they did fall in love, and they stayed together for decades. Not all of us can say the same thing, though. I'm relieved Forest won't marry my daughter if he wouldn't have been able to love her. It will be the best thing for both of them."

They stepped into the elevator. Ellery was at a loss as to what to say. Alpha Young had just told him that his daughter was supposed to marry Forest, but that obviously, now Forest wouldn't marry her because of Ellery. And why hadn't Forest told Ellery about this? Ellery would no doubt have something to say about it as soon as Forest left his mother's side. They'd had hours to talk about this on their way here. Instead of saying something, Forest had babbled about just about everything else.

He was grateful when the alpha stayed silent until they reached the cafeteria. Ellery didn't like this place—he didn't like hospitals, not after what his mother had gone through. She might have been saved if Alpha Carter had allowed her to get cured, but of course, he hadn't. He hadn't allowed any of them to leave pride territory, and Ellery's mother had died. For whatever reason, he hated hospitals now. They represented his dashed hope and everything he'd lost.

He and Alpha Young settled at one of the tables with their coffee. It tasted terrible, but it was warm, and Ellery wrapped his fingers around his cup.

"You're angry with him," Alpha Young said.

"With Forest? I'm *pissed*. He never told me anything about Marissa or what his parents expected from him."

"I'm not saying you shouldn't be angry with him. He hid something big from you. But try to put yourself in his shoes. This is something that was expected from him ever since he was a child. His parents came to talk to me the first time when he was about thirteen or fourteen. I agreed to arrange the marriage because even at that age, I knew he would be a good leader. He and Marissa were friends, and they were close, so I thought it would be for the best. That's what Forest grew up with. Everyone expected him and Marissa to get married and for him to take my place once I stepped down. It's a lot of expectations to put on the shoulders of a young teenager, and it didn't become easier as he grew up. I wasn't surprised when he decided to work for the council and travel around the country. I thought he would come back eventually, but obviously, I was wrong."

Ellery wasn't sure he was. What would have happened if Forest and Ellery hadn't met? Would Forest have continued working for the council, or would he eventually have gone home to marry Marissa? Ellery didn't have an answer to that, and he wasn't sure he wanted one. No matter how angry he was with Forest, he couldn't imagine his mate having to get married to someone he didn't love, especially a woman. He didn't know if Forest was gay, bisexual, or something else, but Ellery supposed it was normal for him to have a hard time imagining his mate with a woman. It didn't matter, though. Forest wouldn't marry Marissa. They would never be together, and that might cause tension in Forest's relationship with his parents.

No doubt that was why he hadn't told Ellery about it. He didn't want to fight with him, too. Ellery would have appreciated being warned, but with everything that was happening, he needed to wait to tear his mate a new one.

"I'm happy he found you," Alpha Young said, startling Ellery out of his thoughts.

"Are you? I mean, my presence in Forest's life just about ruined all your plans."

"Maybe it did, but as long as you and Forest are happy, I think everything will be okay."

"Even with his parents? Because his father didn't look happy when Forest told him I'm his mate."

The alpha grimaced. "It will take a while. I won't hide that from you. Especially with his mother. I love Diane, but she can be difficult, and she will use her heart attack as an excuse."

That sounded more like she would use it as a weapon to make Forest feel guilty. Ellery hoped Forest would see through it, but he couldn't be sure, and he was starting to wonder if he'd done the right thing coming here. He wanted to support his mate, but he didn't want Forest to get hurt by his presence. He didn't want to know what was going to happen if Forest chose Marissa and his parents instead of him. Only an hour ago, he wouldn't have thought it possible, but now, he wasn't that sure anymore. It was a big thing to ask

Forest to choose between him and his parents, and he didn't know which one Forest would choose.

Forest's mother looked much better than Forest had expected. It was both a relief and a reason for him to feel anxious.

She was sitting in her bed, talking with the nurse, and she sounded combative, to say the least. The nurse looked one second away from strangling her, and she huffed on her way out, giving Forest a glance that said *better you than me.*

"Stay in your bed," she told Forest's mother. "I'll check in on you in half an hour. You need rest, not to walk around, and no, you're not going home today, so stop asking." The door slammed behind her, making Forest wince.

He would rather be anywhere but here, but there was no way to avoid it. This was his mother, and she'd had a heart attack. He needed to be with her, even though he knew that she would be pissed about Ellery's presence once she found out about it.

"Forest!" she said when she saw him. She struggled to get out of bed, and Forest rushed to her side, gently pushing her back against the pillows.

"Where do you think you're going?"

"I want to hug my son. Don't tell me I can't do that."

Forest wouldn't tell her she couldn't do anything. He wasn't that stupid. "The nurse told you to stay in bed. You should obey, at least for a while."

She huffed and crossed her arms over her chest. "I don't like that nurse."

That much had been obvious, but Forest ignored it. "She's here to make you feel better. Give her a break, yeah?"

His mother beamed at him. "I'll give her a break only because I'm so happy. I wasn't sure you'd come. I thought maybe you would want to move right away and that you would need some time. So? When are you moving back? When can we pick the day for the wedding? I can't wait to go shopping with Marissa. I thought maybe a late summer wedding? It doesn't make sense for us to wait any longer."

Forest blinked. He'd expected his mother to use her illness against him, but as it was, she was assuming that he'd already decided to move back and get married. He didn't know how to tell her none of that would happen without hurting her. His father had told him she needed to avoid stress, and that was what Forest was about to give her — more stress.

He hated to disappoint her, but he couldn't hide Ellery from her, especially not now that his father knew about him.

"And we can choose a house together," she continued. "I've had my eye on one of them for a while, and it needs some renovations, but I'm sure it will be perfect. There are five bedrooms, so you and Marissa can start having children right away. Oh, I can't wait to have grandchildren. I hope the first one will be a girl, although of course I understand it would be better if it were a boy. You can teach him all about being an alpha."

Forest needed to nip this in the bud before she planned his entire life.

He cleared his throat and looked at his father for help, but his dad was looking away. Forest was pretty sure he could see a smile playing on his lips, and he didn't know what it meant. He couldn't ask, either. Right now, he needed to focus on his mother. "Mom? Slow down," he said.

She glared at him. "How can I slow down? My baby is finally coming home. God, I wish you'd done this years ago. I missed you so much."

Forest winced. He'd known his parents missed him, of course. He missed them, too, but he still thought that staying away had been the best thing for him and that it would continue to be. He had to tell his mother, though. That was *not* going to be fun. "Mom, I know you're happy to see me, but you can't start planning my entire life for me. I'm not moving back."

She blinked, clearly not having expected him to push back. "What do you mean, you're not moving back? Marissa can't move out to wherever you are right now. Her father needs her, and he needs you, too."

"I don't want to stress you out because I know it's important that you stay calm, but I'm not moving, and I'm not marrying Marissa."

She put a hand on her chest, right over her heart, and Forest sucked in a breath. Had he hurt her? Had he stressed her too much? Was she having a second heart attack?

"Of course you have to move back and marry Marissa. It's your duty. It's for the family, and the pack," she said.

Forest grimaced. Apart from the illness, this was the next best thing to make Forest feel guilty about not doing what she wanted.

He knew she always thought he'd eventually come back. He had, too, even though he'd been wary because he'd never wanted to marry Marissa, not even when they were fourteen and he was still figuring out that he preferred men over women. But now, he was here, and Ellery was, too. He couldn't back down. He didn't *want* to back down.

He was surprisingly okay with that. The pack was his past, while the pride was the future. He didn't know how to tell his mom that and about Ellery without having her freak out, though. He didn't want to provoke a second heart attack or something like that.

"Diane," Forest's father said with a sigh. He moved next to his wife and took her hand.

They weren't mates. Forest had always known that. He'd also always known that they were in love, though. They loved each other deeply, and before he realized he could say no to the arranged marriage, he'd hoped that he and Marissa would eventually have the same thing. Now, he knew they wouldn't because he'd met Ellery, and he was in love with him.

"He won't come back," his father said.

"He has to. I don't know what the two of you are talking about."

"He's not coming back. He has a job as the beta of a pride, and he met his mate. He'll never marry Marissa."

Forest pressed his lips together. His father wouldn't have told his mom about all of this if he hadn't thought she could take it, but Forest was still nervous. He watched his mother, looking for signs that she was having another heart attack. He wasn't quite sure what the signs were, though. She was gaping, looking from Forest to his father, her face suddenly pale. All of that could be because of what his father had just said, and Forest didn't want to call the nurse if it wasn't necessary.

"What do you mean, he met his mate?"

"Just that. He's here with his mate."

Forest's mother stopped looking at him, and he felt horrible. He'd hurt her, even though he knew this was the best thing to do for himself. She looked at his father again, her eyes wide. "But we've been talking about this marriage for years. It's all decided."

Forest's father patted her hand. "I know, dear. But you know that having met his mate is more important than an arranged marriage. Forest wants to be with him."

Forest's mother made a strangled sound. "Him?" She looked at Forest again. "You mean you won't even give me any grandkids?"

Forest almost laughed in her face. "I don't know, Mom. Ellery and I haven't talked about that yet. We only met recently, and there's still time."

"Neither of you can have children," she pointed out.

"I know. It doesn't mean we can't adopt or have children

in other ways. If that's your only worry, you shouldn't think about it too much." Hopefully, it was because it would be something that was fairly easy to solve, as long as Ellery wanted kids, too. Forest hadn't thought he did until recently, but he could see him and Ellery raising a small family. Maybe one child, or two at the most. He didn't know, but he and Ellery had their entire life to make that kind of decision.

That was, if Ellery decided to speak to Forest ever again after what Forest had pulled. He should have told Ellery about the arranged marriage and that his parents would expect him to move back. Instead, he'd taken the easy way out, and he'd kept his mouth shut. He'd also left Ellery alone outside with Alpha Young, and that couldn't be good, either. Hopefully, Ellery would understand. Forest hadn't been ready to have this conversation with him, not when he was worried about his mother. He knew he was about to be yelled at, though. Ellery could be passionate, and he'd be in his right to yell at Forest for not telling him this kind of information. It was important, and Forest should have.

His mother shook her head. "I don't understand. We always planned that you would come back and marry Marissa. What are you going to do now?"

"I'm going to stay in Green Hill, Mom. I'll be the permanent beta, and I'll be happy with Ellery." Forest had always known that his parents wanted him to be happy, but right now, he wasn't sure whether or not it was linked with doing what they wanted. He hoped they wouldn't push him away, but he couldn't be entirely sure about that. He didn't know what he would do if they told him they never wanted to see him unless he did what they wanted. Go back home to Green Hill with Ellery, of course, but would he ever be able to heal this wound if it was inflicted?

CHAPTER SIX

It was time to talk. Ellery had been expecting this since he and Forest had arrived, but with Forest's mother still in the hospital, they'd waited. Forest had tried talking to Ellery a few times over the past couple of days, but Ellery had brushed him off. He didn't want to talk. He didn't want to know why Forest hadn't told him about Marissa and his parents' plan. But now, he couldn't ignore Forest any longer.

Forest's father, Paul, had left the house to pick up Diane. Ellery wasn't looking forward to being in the house with both of them—being only with Paul had been hard enough, and he hadn't spent a lot of time there since he'd been mostly at the hospital. But now Diane was coming home, and that meant she'd be there. Ellery hadn't met her yet, and he wished he could go home.

Maybe he should. He could contact a Nix or even Liam and Gal. He knew Liam would come and get him if he wanted him to. He felt like he owed Forest a conversation, though. That was why he was waiting for him in Forest's childhood bedroom, where he'd been sleeping for the past couple of nights.

A knock on the door told him it was time. He was sitting on Forest's bed, trying to come up with a way to avoid this and knowing he couldn't. He sucked in a breath. "Come in," he called out.

Forest had been sleeping on the couch, mostly because he'd wanted to avoid his father's displeasure. Even though Forest and Ellery had never shared a bed, Ellery had been disappointed. He understood where Forest was coming from, but this would have been a good moment to show his father that he was serious about Ellery. Instead, he'd given Ellery his childhood bedroom and he'd stuck to the couch, putting more distance between them. The rest of the distance had been put there by Ellery. He wasn't going to deny that. It wasn't his fault that he was uncomfortable with all of this, though.

The door opened, and Forest looked in. "Can we talk?" he asked.

There it was. Ellery resisted the urge to say no and waved Forest inside. "How long is it going to take your father to come back?"

"I'd say at least a few hours." Forest stepped in and closed the door. "My mother is a little complicated."

From what Ellery had heard about her, that was an understatement. "What do you want to talk about?"

Forest frowned. "You already know what I want to talk about."

"Oh, you mean the fact that your parents expected you to marry the alpha's daughter."

Forest rubbed the back of his neck. "I should have told you sooner. I know that."

"Oh, you know that. I'm so relieved."

Forest arched a brow. "I never realized you were this snarky."

"Maybe it's because we barely spend any amount of time together. I don't even know why I'm here." It wasn't fair. Ellery was here to support Forest, and that wouldn't change, no matter what Forest was about to tell him. He knew Forest didn't want what his parents wanted. He didn't want Marissa. He wanted Ellery.

That didn't make it easier for Ellery to accept, though. Forest had hidden something big from him, and it made him feel vulnerable. He already felt too much that way from being in a place he didn't know, sitting in the home of people who didn't like him.

Forest sighed and stepped closer, but he didn't touch Ellery. "I just wanted to talk about the arranged marriage. I'd already decided not to marry Marissa, and now I know I never want to be a pack member again."

Ellery rubbed his face. He was tired because he hadn't been sleeping well, but this conversation was important, and he needed to focus. "But you never told your parents you weren't coming back."

"You're right. I didn't. I didn't want to. I was afraid of their reaction. I love them, but I always knew they were a bit extreme, especially my mother. You know she hasn't even talked to me since I arrived. I went to the hospital every day, but she barely even looked at me."

"She's angry at you because, out of nowhere, you told her that you had a mate and that you weren't coming back or marrying Marissa."

"Exactly. She would have reacted this way even if I'd told her sooner. I didn't want to face it, and since I was alone, I guess I didn't see the need to do it right away. I would have eventually. I just didn't expect to want to settle down in Green Hill, and I certainly didn't expect to meet you."

Ellery was relieved. He couldn't deny that it had been a big worry for him. Even though Forest had told his father in front of Alpha Young that he wasn't marrying Marissa, Ellery hadn't been able to help but wonder if that was the case. What would Forest gain by not doing this? He would be able to be with Ellery, and to be the beta of the Green Hill pride, but would that be enough? Ellery hadn't wanted to talk to Forest about it, but maybe he should have. If anything, it would have made him feel better about all of this.

He was still worried. He didn't want to force Forest to choose. How could he believe Forest had already decided not to come back? Was Forest saying it only to make Ellery feel better?

"I promise I'd already made this decision," Forest repeated. "I don't like Marissa, not that way, and she doesn't, either. We've always known that."

"But neither of you ever said anything about it to your parents. What were you waiting for? The wedding day?"

Forest chuckled nervously. "We would have stopped it before then, but I get where you're coming from. You're afraid I'm lying to you."

Ellery shook his head. "Not exactly. I'm afraid you'll resent me because I'm making you choose. If you hadn't met me, you could have come back and taken care of your mother, married Marissa, if that was what you wanted, or maybe not married her but still become the next alpha. Alpha Young likes you, and he respects you. He thought you were going to take his place eventually, and being an alpha is better than being a beta."

Forest snorted. "It's not. Trust me. I've had to be an alpha a few times, and I hated it. I see what Gal is doing, and I'm happy I'm not in his place. I like talking with people. I like being a point of referral for the pride members. They don't go to Gal because they don't know him and he's intimidating, but things are different with me. They don't mind talking to me and telling me whatever's wrong. I don't have as much on my shoulders as a beta, and that's very good for me. I'm not a responsibility kind of guy. I'll leave those to Gal, and I'll take care of the rest."

Ellery wanted to believe Forest. He *should* believe him. "So you're a hundred percent sure? Even if you don't consider the alpha position, you could be closer to your parents if you came back."

"That's exactly why I *don't* want to come back. I love my parents. I know you lost your mother and your relationship with your father was impacted by what he did to Liam, so I get why you'd think I'd want to be with mine. I love them, and that won't ever change. But you know my father a bit now. You don't know my mother, but trust me, I do. If I stayed, she would work on me, make me feel guilty, until I did what she wants. I don't want that to happen. I don't want to feel guilty, because I'm not doing anything I should feel guilty for. So what if I don't want to marry Marissa or stay here? They might think that it's my duty to the family, but I don't. I want to be free. I want to do what I want and be with whoever I want." He paused and looked at Ellery. "And that's you. I want to be with you, no one else. Certainly not Marissa."

"We could both move here?" Ellery asked even though he hadn't planned to say that. He didn't want to move. Green Hill might have been a prison for him until recently, but it was still his home, even with Anne probably planning to strip the flesh from his bones or something.

"No offense, but my mother would eat you for breakfast. I don't want you to think you have to avoid her, but again, I know her. She won't be a good person to be around, at least for a little while. She won't stop pushing until I stand my ground, and you and the pride are it for me. I mean that. I'm ready to bond with you, if that's what you want, so that you can believe me."

Ellery blinked. He hadn't expected that. "You want to bond with me so I'll know you won't leave me?"

"No. I want to bond with you because I want to bond with you. I know you're it for me. I know I'll spend the rest of my life with you, trying my best to make you happy even though we've had a rocky start. But if it makes you feel better, if it makes you believe me and that I won't leave you, we can bond right now. I understand that my word might not be enough for you to trust me."

Ellery didn't want to bond because of not trusting Forest.

It wasn't even that he didn't trust him. He just hated the thought of having his mate choose between his family and him.

But Forest had already made his decision, hadn't he? He wanted Ellery, and he'd chosen him. Bonding wouldn't change that, but Forest wasn't wrong when he said it would make Ellery more comfortable. Once they were bonded, he would know that Forest wasn't going anywhere. It might not be the right reason to do it, but it also wasn't a reason *not* to do it.

Ellery nodded. "All right. We can bond. Right now."

Forest had expected Ellery to tell him to fuck off. He would have told himself to fuck off if he'd been in Ellery's place, and with the way Ellery had been avoiding Forest, Forest wouldn't have been surprised. But instead, the most incredible words had come out of Ellery's mouth.

"Are you sure?" Forest asked.

Ellery rolled his eyes. "Why shouldn't I be?"

"Well, it's a bit sudden. We haven't talked about it, and as you pointed out earlier, we haven't spent a lot of time together. We barely know each other."

Ellery's eyes narrowed. "Have you already changed your mind? Do you have doubts? Because I don't. I don't care that we only met recently. We have the rest of our lives to get to know each other. Besides, you were going to marry a woman you could never love. How is it different?"

Forest wasn't sure how to answer that. He didn't want Ellery to be angry at him. Now that Ellery had agreed to bond with him, he didn't want to do anything to make him change his mind. "I never said I would marry Marissa."

"But you might have. You certainly thought that your parents would push you into it. That's the reason you stayed away, isn't it?"

"It is."

"And from what Alpha Young told me, your parents aren't mates. Theirs is an arranged marriage, too. Yet they learned to live with each other, and they fell in love."

"You're right. I don't think that two people in an arranged marriage can't love each other. But you and I are different. We're mates."

"Exactly. That means that we'll definitely fall in love, doesn't it? It's not an arranged marriage." Ellery paused. "It's not one, at all. But we already know we fit together well. We already know that we'll fall in love. Why wait?"

Forest sat next to Ellery. "You're afraid I'll disappear, aren't you?" Ellery had already lost so much. His mother had died, then his father had been arrested. Most of the pride didn't like him. He didn't have much, and Forest wasn't sure he'd been happy before. Hell, he wasn't sure Ellery was happy now.

Ellery shrugged. "A bit. But does it really matter? I'm convinced that we'll eventually fall in love. I like you, Forest. Nothing is going to change that."

"Are you sure you like me? Because you don't seem to be very happy with me."

To Forest's surprise, Ellery leaned closer and kissed his cheek. "I might not be happy with you right now, but it doesn't mean I don't like you. Besides, I understand where you're coming from. I understand why you hid all of this from your family, and why you're so hesitant. They're your parents. You love them, and you don't want to disappoint them. But there comes a time when you might have to, and this could be that time. They can't live your life for you. You're the one making these decisions, not them. You have to choose between the future they planned for you and the future you want. I understand why you're hesitant, but it doesn't change anything."

Forest wasn't hesitant. He'd chosen Ellery, and he would never go back. "Okay. Let's bond."

They stared at each other for a moment, then Forest laughed. "It's not romantic or sexy."

"It doesn't need to be. I mean, we don't have to have sex to bond."

Forest arched a brow. "I don't know about you, but I've wanted to have sex with you since the first time I saw you. Unless you don't want to?"

Ellery's cheeks flushed. "It's not that I don't want to. But you know how isolated the pride was. You know I couldn't leave the house. I have some experience, but it's been a while, and I'm nervous."

That broke Forest's heart a little. He took Ellery in his arms and pulled him close, kissing the tip of his nose. "I don't care how nervous you are. I am, too. I want this to be perfect for us, but I know that first times rarely are. But no matter what happens, no matter how much I fuck this up, I know you're not going anywhere, and it makes things easier."

Ellery swallowed heavily, and Forest followed the rise and fall of his Adam's apple. He waited for Ellery to make a decision, smiling when Ellery swung himself around and straddled Forest's lap. It reminded Forest of the time in his office, and he couldn't wait to get his hands on Ellery — properly this time. He wanted Ellery naked against him, but they had to hurry. "My parents won't be gone for long," he murmured, burying his face against Ellery's neck.

"It's a good thing I have lube in my bag, then."

Forest barked out a laugh. He hadn't expected that, but he liked it. Ellery was an odd mix of conflicting particularities, sometimes hesitant yet also forceful and sure of himself. It would take time for Forest to learn and understand him, and he couldn't wait.

"Are you sure you want to do this now?" Ellery asked.

"I wouldn't have suggested it otherwise."

"But we both know your parents, especially your mother, aren't going to be happy about this."

Forest leaned back. "You're right. She's probably going to yell at me. But you're also right when you say that I have to decide if I want to live their future or mine, and I've already made this decision. *You* are my future, Ellery. I'm never going to change my mind about that."

Ellery stared at Forest for a moment, then grabbed the bottom of his t-shirt. Forest held his arms up and helped Ellery get rid of it, then of his. Once they were naked chest against naked chest, Forest wanted more. He knew they didn't have a lot of time, and he wanted to make the most out of it. He hated that they were rushing this, but if they wanted to do it now, they couldn't waste time. He would have to be careful, because he didn't want to hurt Ellery.

The thought made him stop. "What do you want?" he asked.

"Would you let me fuck you if that was what I wanted?" Ellery asked, his voice quiet.

"Of course." Forest usually was the one doing the fucking, but he was ready to do pretty much anything for his mate. He didn't hate bottoming. He wasn't crazy about it, but he suspected that had more to do with his past experiences than with the act itself. He would try at least once with Ellery, and they would go from there. Maybe today wasn't the perfect day to do that, but if that was what Ellery wanted, Forest wouldn't say no. "Is that what you want?"

Ellery shook his head and got to his feet. "Stay here," he said, pushing Forest back when he tried to follow him.

Forest looked at Ellery as he moved around the room, going to his bag and opening a side pocket. He grinned when he saw the bottle of lube Ellery had been hiding, and even though Ellery had told him to stay where he was, he got to his feet and quickly pushed down his jeans and underwear. He didn't have time to take off his shoes, socks, and pants, but the jeans pooled at his feet, and that was enough. His dick was out, hard and brushing against his stomach as he sat back on the bed and watched Ellery. Ellery never stopped moving. He took his clothes off quickly and functionally, and Forest almost swallowed his tongue at the sight.

This was his mate, and he was the most beautiful person Forest had ever seen. Forest couldn't wait to get his hands on him, and he opened his arms, silently beckoning Ellery to come back.

Ellery did. He was still hesitant, but there was a fire in his gaze, and Forest couldn't wait to burn himself on it.

"I like it when you take control like this," Forest murmured as Ellery settled back in his lap and opened the lube.

"Do you?"

"Yeah. I'm always in control, you know? People come to me when they have a problem and expect me to solve it. They expect me to take charge. It's nice not to have to sometimes."

"It's only because I'm with you. I don't think I'd be able to behave like this with anyone else. But I trust you, and I know that if I do something you don't like, you'll tell me. I know that even if I'm ridiculous, you won't laugh at me, but rather, with me."

Forest didn't like that Ellery might feel ridiculous, but he was glad Ellery trusted him so much. He ran his hands down Ellery's sides and cupped his ass. "Nothing you do is ridiculous. If anything, it's fucking hot. I can't wait to get inside you, and I love that you are in charge even though you'll be the one getting fucked."

Ellery chuckled. "Topping from the bottom, right?"

"I'd like nothing more."

Forest continued running his hands over Ellery's body as

Ellery reached behind himself. Forest knew what Ellery was doing, and it was even sexier than it had been in his mind. Since Ellery didn't ask for his help, he let him take the lead, but he couldn't help but slide his fingers between Ellery's ass cheeks. He swallowed heavily when his fingertips brushed against the place where Ellery's fingers entered his hole. He was moving them in and out, and Forest followed the movement. On the next thrust inside, he added one of his fingers.

Ellery made a strangled sound, and Forest froze, but Ellery didn't. If anything, he moved faster, pushing his cock against Forest's stomach. Forest wrapped his other hand around it, jacking Ellery off until Ellery shook his head and pushed him away.

Forest let go immediately, wondering what he'd done wrong, but he realized the answer was *nothing*.

"Stop that. You're going to make me come, and I don't want that to happen until you're inside me," Ellery murmured.

He took his fingers—and Forest's—out of his hole, then wrapped them around Forest's dick. Forest sucked in a breath. He had a hard time believing he was already this close to coming, but he supposed he shouldn't be surprised. Ellery was his mate, and every single move he made was so fucking sexy that Forest couldn't help but wonder how long he was going to last.

Sliding inside Ellery was heaven. Forest was pretty sure his eyes rolled back in his head, and he clutched at Ellery's ass, trying to pull him even closer. That was impossible, though. He needed to let Ellery set the pace, so he loosened his hold and prayed that it wouldn't take Ellery too long. He knew it could take a while for Ellery's body to get used to the invasion, and he held his breath, letting Ellery move at his own pace.

When Ellery was finally sitting on his thighs with his cock

entirely buried his body, Forest finally let go of his breath.

"You're tense," Ellery said.

"You'd be tense in my place, too. Can you move? Please?" Forest didn't even care that he sounded like he was begging. He might as well have been.

Ellery nodded, and to Forest's relief, raised his body. Forest didn't want to push Ellery too far too fast, but he couldn't help but push his hips up every time Ellery came down. They found an easy rhythm they both could follow without hurting each other, and Forest grunted every time Ellery dropped on his thighs and buried his cock inside him.

"If you want to bond, you should probably do it now," Ellery murmured.

He sounded like he was giving Forest an easy way out, but it was a way out Forest didn't want or need. He nodded, eyeing Ellery's neck, already knowing where he would bite him. His fangs had popped out a while ago, and they ached with the need to bury themselves inside their mate, too.

So Forest did it. He leaned closer, briefly breathing in Ellery's scent, and bit him. Ellery's blood filled his mouth, and even though it wasn't exactly the best taste in the world, Forest was happy. This was exactly what he'd wanted since the first time he met Ellery, even though he hadn't been sure he would ever be able to have it. But he did now, and he hoped neither of them would regret it. He knew he wouldn't. He was sure of that.

He barely felt it when Ellery bit him, too. There was no pain, only pleasure, so much pleasure that Forest had never felt like this in his entire life. He knew it wouldn't happen again, but that was okay. The next time he and Ellery would have sex, they would already be bonded. It would be different, but just as good.

Forest quivered as Ellery's movements picked up. He continued drinking Ellery's blood until he had to close his eyes, pleasure becoming the center of his world. It exploded in his groin and behind his eyelids, and he couldn't resist anymore. He filled Ellery's ass, screwing his eyes shut as the pleasure took over.

Maybe it was a good thing that it wouldn't be like this ever again. He was pretty sure he'd die if it felt like this every time they made love.

Warmth splashed on his stomach, and he knew Ellery had come, too. The bond was complete, sealed, and it filled Forest's soul in a way nothing else had.

For the first time in Forest's life, he felt complete, and that was only because of Ellery.

They stayed wrapped around each other for as long as they could. Ellery wished they were at home in Green Hill so they could stay in the room for the rest of the day. But they weren't, and he had to face Forest's parents. There was no way Ellery wanted to be naked when they came back, so he only allowed himself fifteen minutes to bask in the knowledge that he and Forest were one. They had bonded and would spend the rest of their lives together.

That was, if neither of them did something stupid. They would probably want to strangle each other eventually, but for some reason, that didn't scare Ellery as much as it would have any other day. They could do this. They could be together and make each other happy. He was sure of that, even though he wasn't sure of much in his life.

He kissed Forest's naked shoulder and rose from the bed. Forest tried to keep him there, but Ellery playfully glared at him. "What's going to happen when your parents come back and we're naked in your bed?"

"They don't come in the bedroom. I'm sure they know better."

Ellery *wasn't* sure, especially when it came to Forest's mother, so he ignored the way Forest try to pull him back and cleaned up before getting dressed. Forest huffed and whined, but he followed Ellery's lead, and Ellery was grateful when they heard the front door open only ten minutes later.

He shot Forest a meaningful glance, and Forest had the good sense to look sheepish. Forest headed toward the door, pausing after he opened it and offering Ellery his hand. "Ready to face the music?" he asked.

Ellery didn't think he'd ever be ready, but he nodded anyway as he took Forest's hand.

Together, they walked down the stairs.

Ellery knew this conversation wouldn't be an easy one, but it had to be done. He still wished it didn't have to be when Forest's mother was just coming back from the hospital, but they couldn't hang around forever. They had a life to go back to in Green Hill, and after what had just happened, Ellery couldn't wait.

He half expected to be kicked out of the house, especially when he and Forest appeared holding hands. He was pretty sure Forest's mother, who glared at him, wished she could make him disappear, but to his surprise and relief, she stayed silent.

"Forest," Paul said when he noticed them. "Why don't you help me?"

He was holding two bags and his wife, and Ellery wondered how he managed to keep his balance.

Forest let go of Ellery's hand to grab the two bags and put them on the floor next to the stairs. As soon as that was done, he took Ellery's hand again, and Ellery clutched his fingers. He was nervous, and they weren't even his parents. He could only imagine how Forest felt.

"You're both here," Forest's mother said as her husband helped her to the couch.

"Of course we are," Forest answered. "We wanted to wait for you to come home before heading back to Green Hill."

"You're already leaving?"

Forest's expression hardened just a bit, but enough that Ellery knew he was serious about this. "We have to go back, Mom. As much as I loved seeing you, I have a job to go back to."

She sighed heavily. "I was hoping you would stay a bit longer."

"We already talked about that. Ellery and I will come back as soon as we can."

Ellery wondered why she wasn't kicking him out, but he wasn't about to ask. She glared at him as if she could do it with a thought, and he was extremely uncomfortable. The fact that it hurt when he sat down also didn't help, and he made a mental note not to have sex with Forest before an important conversation. He was pretty sure Diane would realize what had happened if he tried finding a more comfortable seat, so he did his best to stay still as he and Forest sat on the couch opposite Diane. Paul sat next to his wife and took one of her hands, and they faced each other, couple against couple.

Paul sighed. "This is it, then," he said.

"You already knew this would happen," Forest pointed out. "I love you and Mom, and I wish I could be the son you want, but I'm not. I'm me, and I want Ellery. I could never have married Marissa, and I should have told you that sooner. I'm sorry. I was afraid to disappoint you."

Ellery shouldn't be here for this conversation, but he doubted Forest would let him go if he tried to leave. Forest was still holding his hand, and he was clutching it almost to the point of pain. Ellery could feel Forest was uncomfortable, but also insecure and scared, and even though Forest hadn't told him about it, he knew why. Forest loved his parents, and he wished he could do what they wanted. He was terrified that they would reject him now that he wasn't.

Ellery doubted that would be the case, but how could he be sure? They weren't his parents. They were Forest's.

"You should have waited," Diane said.

"What do you mean?"

"This isn't the moment. I just came home from the hospital. I'm still fragile, and —"

Paul snorted so loud that his wife glared at him. He shook his head and looked at Forest. "Don't listen to her. She might have just left the hospital, but that doesn't mean she's not okay. She is. The doctor is positive that with a change in diet and less stress, she'll live to see her grandchildren, and possibly her great-grandchildren."

"What grandchildren?" Diane asked. "Neither of them can carry a child."

Ellery stiffened, but thankfully, Forest took the lead. "It doesn't mean we can't have children, though. You know that."

"Not blood-related children."

"Does it matter? Would you care if my child had my blood running in his veins or not? Besides, it's not like we have to adopt. We could use a surrogate." He paused and looked at Ellery, and Ellery would have smiled at the sudden panic he could feel swelling in Forest in any other situation. "I'm not saying we should have children. I know we haven't spoken about it yet, and I don't want you to think you have to do anything."

Ellery leaned closer and kissed Forest's cheek. "I'm not opposed to children. Don't worry. We should talk about it first, though."

The relief in Forest was intense, and Ellery couldn't help but stay close to him. He could feel Diane's glare on him, but he didn't care. She wasn't the one he had to be there for. Forest was, and he would do what any other mate would do his place.

"Even if we ignore the children part, what about every-thing we've already organized for the wedding?"

Forest frowned. "What do you mean? We never even picked a date. Besides, you know Marissa and I were never more than friends."

"But you would have been such a cute couple."

"Because Ellery and I aren't?" Forest sucked in a breath. "Look, Mom, I love you. That will never change. But if you want me in your life, you're going to have to accept Ellery. You have to accept that I will never marry Marissa and that my life is in Green Hill now, with Ellery. If you can't accept that, if you can't behave like a normal mother-in-law to him, then you'll eventually lose me. I don't want that to happen, but I won't subject him to your glares and whining. It's not an ultimatum. I never want to give you one. But this is what's going to happen if you continue behaving this way with him. You're my mother, but he's my mate, and he means a lot to me. I hope you'll realize that before something between us breaks."

Forest wasn't surprised when his mother's lower lip trem-bled. "So you're just going to abandon us?" she asked.

He'd expected that question. He'd expected her to try to play with his emotions. She always did. He knew she didn't mean it like a bad thing—she wanted him to stay because she loved him and she wanted to make sure he was happy. But she didn't understand that having to stick around when he didn't want to was the exact opposite.

"I'm not abandoning you and Dad," he told her. "I know I won't live next door, but it's not that far away. Especially with Nix easily available now, it won't be a problem for me to come back as often as you need me to." He should be careful with what he promised, otherwise his mom would ask him to come back to open a jar of pickles, but right now, he knew she needed this. If she overstepped, he could always put her back in the boundaries.

"I always thought you would come back," she whined.

"And I will. Just not permanently. I'm sorry, Mom, but my life is in Green Hill now."

"What kind of pride has a wolverine beta?" his father asked.

Again, Forest wasn't surprised. His mother used emotions. His father tended to use logic. "A pride who needs one. I told you about Green Hill. They went through a lot with their old alpha and beta, and they deserve better. They *have* better now, with Gal in charge."

"And they accept you? Even though you're not the same kind of shifter as they are?"

Forest wasn't offended. The pack only had wolverine shifters. It wasn't because they didn't want other kinds of shifters, but rather because they were old fashioned, as the arranged marriage tradition showed. Besides, even if they had other kinds of shifters, it would still be weird to have different shifters in positions of power. It wasn't usual. "We're doing good so far. They accepted us, even though it hasn't been easy. And I know it will continue to be hard, but it's my job. I love doing this, and I'm happy to be able to help."

Forest's father cocked his head. "And you're sure you won't regret not being able to continue traveling?"

Forest knew that was also one of Ellery's fears, even though Ellery hadn't mentioned it. If he was honest, it was one of his fears, too. "I think I'll be okay. I don't want to hurt you by saying this, but the main reason I took this job was that I didn't want to be here. I thought that the easiest way to make sure you didn't push me into marrying Marissa was to stay away."

"Instead of talking to us?" There was pain in his voice, and Forest felt guilty.

Forest rubbed the back of his neck. "I know I should have talked to you sooner. I won't deny I did this all wrong. But I need you to understand how hard this was for me. I never wanted to disappoint the two of you. I never wanted you to hate me."

Forest's mother made a strangled sound. "We could never hate you. You're our little boy."

Forest flushed. "But I'm not a boy anymore. I don't do what you want me to do. I really thought you would be angry." And they were. He knew that. "But I can't deny all of this anymore. I can't deny that I met my mate and that I'm happy, and that it's not here."

His mother sighed heavily, and he held his breath, expecting her to start yelling at him or, at the very least, to tell him how disappointed she was. Instead, she nodded curtly. "You're right. I can't say I'm happy about this, but it doesn't mean I hate you. I could never hate you. I *love* you. I only ever wanted the best for you, and I truly believe the best would be to come back here and marry Marissa." She smiled sadly. "But you're also right when you say that you're not my little boy anymore. You're an adult, and you're the one making decisions. I can't force you to do anything, and I won't push you away just because you don't agree with what I think. I don't want to lose you. If that means I have to accept that you're moving to Green Hill permanently and that you have a male mate, then I will." She wrinkled her nose. "Just don't expect this to be easy for me. I've dreamed about your wedding with Marissa and my grandchildren for so long that it's going to take me a bit to get used to the idea that they'll never become reality."

Forest was in shock. He hadn't expected his mother to be so understanding. He'd expected her to scream, to try to manipulate him into staying—and she had, in the beginning. But now, she seemed to have accepted that Forest wasn't going to do what she wanted. It was a surprise, and he wasn't sure how to deal with that.

"The pride has accepted him," Ellery said quietly. He hadn't spoken yet, and Forest hoped it wasn't going to be a disaster, but his parents might as well get used to having Ellery in their life. "Like Forest said, it hasn't been easy. We had a horrible experience with our old alpha. He kept the pride inside the house, and he tried to kidnap one of the members who left. But we're doing better now, and it's thanks to Gal and Forest. We need them."

Forest's father cleared his throat. "Of course. Forest is a good beta. He always has been."

Forest could have laughed. He *was* a good beta, but his parents had never accepted that this was what he wanted to do with his life. They always wanted him to become the alpha.

"He really is. We're grateful for his presence in Green Hill."

"All right, enough of this," Forest said. "I agree I'm a good beta, but I don't need to listen to you praising me." He looked at his parents. "This is what I want to do. I know it's weird for you since, there are only wolverines in our pack, but things are changing out there. Shifters are mixing and creating new groups and families, and that's what's happening in Green Hill. It doesn't matter what kind of shifter I am, or what kind of shifter Ellery is. The pride is doing good, and I want that to continue. That's why I'm going back. Well, one of the reasons."

"Of course," his father agreed.

Forest allowed himself to lean back in his seat and relax. He'd thought this would be so much worse. He'd expected to have a fight on his hands, and he had, but it was nowhere near as bad as he'd expected.

He could do this. He was doing it. It had taken him years,

but he'd finally stood up to his parents, and he was doing what he wanted. He had the pride and Ellery, and that was all he'd ever needed.

He didn't know what the future would be like for him or the pride, but he knew it would be in Green Hill. Whatever happened, he would have Ellery by his side, and that was the thing that made him happiest.

He squeezed Ellery's hand, and Ellery squeezed back. Forest could feel Ellery was still tense and confused, but he wasn't afraid anymore, and Forest was grateful. He wanted his parents and his mate to get along, even though he realized how hard it was to get along with his mother. But if there was one person who could do that, it was Ellery. He was perfect for Forest. He could stand up to Forest's parents, and that was why he was Forest's mate. He'd helped Forest realize that he was strong enough, and Forest hoped he would understand he was, too. But as long as Forest had the three people inside this room in his life, he would be happy.

His mother clapped her hands, making him jump. "All right. When are you two going to get married?"

Forest swallowed. "Get married? Mom, we're mates."

She narrowed her eyes. "So? I don't care what you do in your bedroom or how many times you bite each other. You *have* to have a ceremony. I want to be able to wear my pretty dress, you know, the one I bought for your wedding. I can plan everything, of course. You just have to give me a date."

Forest groaned. His mother was never going to change, was she?

CHAPTER SEVEN

Ellery leaned closer to let him. "Why are we doing this again?" he asked in a whisper.

Liam didn't look at him, keeping his gaze straight ahead. "Because Gal needs a personal assistant."

"And you couldn't do that without me?" Ellery didn't understand why he had to be there. Surely Gal should be the one picking his personal assistant. He didn't need Ellery's help to do that.

Liam's gaze moved to Ellery. "This wouldn't be happening if you'd accepted the job."

"I'm not accepting a job I don't want." Ellery would hate being a personal assistant, even if it were to the alpha. He loved being outside and gardening. That was what he wanted to do with his life. After spending so much time locked inside the house, he wanted out. Besides, it would be kind of a conflict of interest if the beta's mate was the alpha's secretary, wouldn't it?

"I have work to do," Gal grumbled. He was on Liam's other side, and Ellery gave him an understanding glance.

Liam, on the other hand, glared at him. "You can go as soon as you choose one of them."

The three of them were sitting behind Gal's desk, with two pride members sitting on the other side of it—Simon and Kevin. They were the only ones left after Liam had gone through the list of those who had applied to be Gal's assistant.

"I want your opinion," Liam continued. "Who do you think should be Gal's assistant?"

"I wish we weren't doing this in front of them," Ellery murmured. He didn't know either of the men well. They'd spent a lot of time locked in the house, of course, but Ellery had stuck with Liam most of the time. Besides, Alpha Carter hadn't wanted any of them to be friends because he was afraid that they would rise against him. He kept people apart as much as he could, which was why Ellery and Liam weren't close friends. They were working on it, though.

Ellery sighed. How was he supposed to choose the alpha's personal assistant? This wasn't his job. He wanted to go out there and play with Forest, who was waiting for him. Ellery had promised him he would be done soon, but instead, he was still sitting here, and he didn't know what to do. He couldn't pick one of the guys randomly because Liam would know. He had to put some reasoning behind it, and he would probably have to explain it.

"This is your job, not mine," he whispered.

"Please? I trust your judgment. That's all. I want to be sure that Gal's personal assistant is perfect."

"Stop making me feel guilty. Of course I'll help you." Ellery would help every time Liam needed him. He understood how hard this was for him—he had to deal with Sandra, who was still hunting him as often as she could with a list of demands and suggestions about how she thought things should be done. Liam had started avoiding her, but he couldn't always.

And Gal. From what Ellery knew, he was finally done with the accounts. He'd untangled everything, and the pride was in debt with a lot of people. But thanks to the council, they were paying those debts back, and the fact that almost all the pride members had found jobs in town was also helping. There were still a few snags, like the teams who worked in the house, but they would eventually solve all the problems. Besides, as long as Anne stayed as far away from Ellery as she could, Ellery didn't care who cooked or cleaned the communal areas or whatever. He still wished Gal would force her to take a job out of the house, but he wasn't about to ask.

He sighed and looked at the two guys in front of him. They were both nervous, but Kevin was friends with Anne, and that disqualified him as far as Ellery was concerned. He'd never stood up to Anne. He'd stayed there, watching as she insulted Ellery even though Ellery hadn't done anything to deserve it.

Some of the pride members still didn't like him, and Ellery didn't care. He didn't care that Anne wanted to kill him in his sleep. He didn't sleep alone anymore these days, so she wouldn't be able to. She'd have to pass over Forest's body to do that, and Forest wasn't going anywhere. He'd eat her for breakfast if she tried anything, even though his wolverine form was smaller than her tiger form.

Most pride members were finally realizing that Ellery had had nothing to do with what his father had done. They saw how Gal, Liam, and Forest treated him, and they understood. It didn't mean Ellery had forgiven them. He wasn't sure he could, not after everything. But they didn't isolate him as much as they used to except for Anne's small group.

"I say Simon," Ellery said.

Liam wrinkled his nose. "Simon? Are you sure?"

"He's not a bully. That's all I need to know about him."

"I agree," Gal said as he rose from his chair. "Simon? Congratulations. You got the job."

Ellery didn't stay long after that. It had nothing to do with him, even though he'd been there to support Liam. He suspected Gal had already made his decision anyway. Gal and Ellery thought surprisingly alike, and Ellery wasn't surprised that the bullying was what had tilted the balance.

Ellery headed outside, relieved when no one tried to stop him. Forest was at their bench, and Ellery couldn't wait.

He smiled when he approached the bench and saw the

bundle of clothes on one side and the wolverine sleeping on the other. Forest had crawled up on the warm stone and was in wolverine heaven, his nose twitching every so often as he slept. Ellery didn't want to disturb him, so he made sure to be quiet as he took his clothes off and shifted. He would never fit on the bench in his tiger form, so he stretched out on the ground, enjoying the warmth of the sun on his fur.

Something touched the top of his head, and he tilted it to look at the bench. He'd thought Forest was out for the count, but Forest was looking down at him, his gaze sleepy but present. He poked Ellery again, and Ellery showed him his teeth. It wasn't a serious warning, though, so Forest ignored it and jumped on top of Ellery. His wolverine form was smaller and much lighter, so it didn't faze Ellery. He pulled Forest close, snuggling him between his front paws, rubbing his nose against his head. Forest squeaked but didn't try to move away, not until Ellery playfully nipped at his ear.

Ellery let him go. He knew some people found it weird that Forest was the beta yet was the smallest shifter in the pride, but Ellery didn't care. To him, Forest was his mate, and that was what mattered the most.

Forest sniffed at Ellery's face, and Ellery got to his feet. Forest wanted to play, and they didn't have a lot of time to do that, not with the amount of work that still needed to be done.

The roof was fixed, but it didn't mean there weren't another hundred small jobs to do on the house. Forest had to coordinate everyone, including the shifters who worked for the pride, while Ellery had taken his place in the garden with the team that grew some of the food for the pride's kitchen.

It wasn't perfect, but they'd accepted him, and he couldn't be happier. He could have had this even without meeting Forest, but he would never regret letting his mate into his life. He had what he'd always wanted—a family, a pride who finally accepted him, and a freedom he'd never thought he'd find.

He couldn't say that all of it was thanks to Forest, but in part, it was, and as Ellery bounded toward him, he made sure to send love through their bond. He wanted Forest to know how much he cared, even though he wasn't ready yet to say it to Forest's face.

There would be time for that, though. They had their entire life in front of them, and Ellery intended to make the most of it.

YOU MAY ALSO ENJOY THE FOLLOWING FROM EXTASY BOOKS INC:

In Spite of Everything
Catherine Lievens

Excerpt

Kaspar almost collided with Chris outside the kitchen. He managed to step to the side before Chris mowed him over, and he watched Chris as he stomped his way upstairs.

He'd heard the fight. He was pretty sure that everyone in the house and even a few people outside of it had heard it. Fights between Jacob and Chris were almost routine by now, and Kaspar wasn't sure anyone could do anything about them. Things would change once Chris moved back home, but no one knew when that would be, and Kaspar couldn't help but wonder what would happen then.

He looked toward the kitchen, then at the stairs again. Kaspar didn't know where Nico, Chris' brother, was, but it wasn't upstairs. Maybe Chris shouldn't be alone. He might not want to see anyone right now, but Kaspar wanted him to know that he wasn't alone. He had friends who would listen to him if he needed them to. Kaspar wasn't about to take a side because he didn't think anyone was wrong in this situation, but he could support Chris.

He followed Chris upstairs.

Chris' bedroom door was closed, of course, but Kaspar quietly knocked. He was surprised when Chris called at him to enter, then realized Chris had probably thought he was Jacob when Chris' eyes widened and his expression crumbled. He flopped back onto his bed and looked away.

Kaspar stepped in and closed the door behind himself. "I'm sorry if I'm bothering you," he said.

"You're not bothering me. Did you need anything?"

Kaspar hesitated. Chris was strong. Everyone knew that, including Chris. But sometimes, Chris thought that being strong meant that he couldn't show vulnerability. He was already fighting against the fact that he was a carrier and that carriers never became alphas. It hadn't been a law, but carriers had been considered weak until recently. Some people still thought that. The last thing Chris needed was for people to think he was weak because he had emotions.

All of that was bullshit.

"You had a fight with Jacob," Kaspar said.

Chris rolled his eyes. "I'm pretty sure everyone knows about that. We're not exactly quiet when we fight."

"Do you want to talk about it?"

Chris shrugged, and for one moment, he looked like the young man he was. He was younger than Kaspar by six years, way too young to become alpha. Luckily for him, that wouldn't happen anytime soon. It didn't mean he didn't have responsibilities, though.

"My father wants me and Nico to go home," Chris said.

"You already knew this would happen."

"I knew this would happen from the time I got here. That's not the problem."

"Jacob is."

Chris laughed darkly. "He definitely is. I never expected to fall in love when I got here. Hell, I thought I would hate it. I didn't want to leave home. I didn't want to hide, and I thought I was strong enough to face the council and everyone else."

"Hiding doesn't mean you're not strong."

"I know. But I thought I couldn't show people that I was afraid."

Kaspar wasn't sure if Chris had shown had ever anyone he was afraid, but he didn't point that out. Chris was talking to him, and that was the important thing. "You didn't expect Jacob."

"I didn't. I thought that once the carriers were safe, Nico and I would go home and go back to our lives. That's what my father wants me to do. He wants me to go home so he can continue teaching me how to be the next alpha."

"And that's what you want, too."

Chris bit his lower lip. "I've always known I couldn't stay here forever. I'm not a badger shifter."

"You know Thomas doesn't care about that." If anything, the badger alpha had been collecting shifter species. Two of his sons were married to bear shifters, while another was married to a weasel shifter. That wasn't all. The carriers in this house all belonged to a different shifter species who shared the forest with the badgers.

"Can you imagine my father's face if I told him I want to stay?" Chris snorted. "I don't think so. Besides, I always expected to go home. I didn't think I would fall in love with Jacob, though." He raked a hand through his hair. "Or for Jacob to be this stubborn."

"You're stubborn, too," Kaspar pointed out.

Chris smiled at him. "You're right. I am. I know I am. But I don't want to leave him. I know I have to go home. My father won't take no for an answer. He expects me to take my rightful place one day, and to do that, I have to know how to lead the pride. I have to learn what he has to teach me. I just don't understand why Jacob won't come with me."

Kaspar took a risk and sat on the edge of Chris' mattress. "Well, the cete needs him more than ever now."

"Why? The carriers are safe."

"For now, sure. But you know there's a human team coming. They're going to look at all of us, including the cete. I wouldn't be surprised if some of the shifters against us tried something with the humans to get rid of Thomas. Besides, not all carriers have a home to go back to. Some of us are staying, and we will need people to protect us."

"Everyone is safe here, though. The Bishop house is far away from the edge of badger territory. I know Thomas is thinking about lowering the number of guards here. The carriers won't be attacked. We have rights now, and everyone knows it."

"There might be new laws in place, but it doesn't mean everyone is going to follow them. Come on, Chris. You know better than that."

"But it's not fair. Why is the cete important than me?"

Kaspar knew he had to be very careful about what he said. "This is his home, his family. It's the place where he grew up, and where he thought he would live for the rest of his life."

"And I get that. I do. But can't he see that being the next alpha is more important?"

"Not to him. You said you want him to go with you?"

"Of course I do."

"And he doesn't want to. Why?"

"Because he doesn't want to be the alpha mate. He doesn't want to leave the cete. I should be more important than that, but I'm not."

"So you're going to break up?"

Chris' eyes widened, and he shook his head. "Of course not. I'm sure we can find a compromise."

"Can you, though? Because it looks to me like neither of you is ready to compromise. And the thing is, I understand where both of you are coming from. Being the next alpha is important to you. It's something you've been groomed to be ever since you were born, and something everyone expects from you. You don't want to disappoint your father. That's noble. But I also understand why Jacob doesn't want to go with you. He never expected to be an alpha mate, and it's not an easy role to slip into. Besides, the two of you aren't married, and we both know that your father won't be happy if he ever finds out about your relationship."

"That's exactly why Jacob should come with me now. He could get used to being my husband and to his role by my side. My father will see that Jacob is the right man for me once he gets to know him."

Kaspar wasn't sure about that. Alpha Wiley loved his sons, and he wanted them to be treated as more than carriers, but that didn't mean he would want his heir to step out of line. He supported the carriers' laws because he wanted Chris and Nico to be respected, but he still wanted Chris to be his heir because it was tradition and how things had gone for decades. "Whatever happens, one or both of you will have to give up a lot."

"I can't give up. Being the next alpha is important. And no for me. It's important for the pride."

"You're right. It's important. But is it more important than Jacob? Because that's what it's going to come down to in the end, isn't it? If you can't convince Jacob to go with you, and it doesn't look like you will, you'll have to choose. Either he is the most important thing in your life, or being the next alpha is."

"Both things are important."

"And I'm not saying it's wrong that you feel that way. In a perfect world, you would have both. In this world, you can't, Chris. You're going to have to choose, and I doubt you'll like the result." Because either way, he would lose something important to him. Kaspar was glad he wasn't in his place, but right now, with Chris looking so tiny and vulnerable, he kind of wished he were. He wanted to take away Chris' pain, but he couldn't.

The only thing he could do was to be there for Chris, and he didn't know how much that would help.

ABOUT THE AUTHOR

Catherine is the creator of several series, most of them paranormal, including the Whitedell Pride Series and the Gillham Pack Series. While she graduated in translation, she decided to go the writer's way because it was more fun to create her own stories and characters.

She's been living in Italy for more than twenty years, but she's a daughter of the North—Belgium to be precise—and she misses it so much that she's already planning to move back.

She loves pizza—probably too much—her son, her pets, and of course, books. She sneaks some reading time into her schedule every time she has five minutes free from writing, demands from her various pets and son, and lastly, housework.

Connect with her:

lievens.catherine@gmail.com
BookBub: https://www.bookbub.com/authors/catherine-lievens
Website: https://authorcatherinelievens.wordpress.com/
Facebook: https://www.facebook.com/catherine.lievens.9
Facebook Group: https://www.facebook.com/groups/411788002341528/
Twitter: https://twitter.com/authorCLievens
Newsletter: http://eepurl.com/c-uvKn

www.ingramcontent.com/pod-product-compliance
Lightning Source LLC
Chambersburg PA
CBHW060629130626
46555CB00002B/728